Yes, Carol...
It's Christmas!

Yes, Carol...

It's Christmas!

by

Cindy Vincent

Whodunit Press
Houston

Yes, Carol . . . It's Christmas!

Published by Whodunit Press

A Division of Mysteries by Vincent, LLC

For information, please contact:

Whodunit Press

c/o Mysteries by Vincent

Mysteriesbyvincent.com

This is a work of fiction. All events, locations, institutions, themes, persons, characters and plot are completely fictional. Any resemblance to places or persons, living or deceased, are of the invention of the author.

ISBN: 978-1-932169-79-9

Printed in the United States of America

Dedication

To all those good-hearted souls who love to make the Christmas season a special time for everyone around them, by putting up lights and decorations, or baking those favorite cookies, or hosting a Christmas party for so many to enjoy . . . May the season and the reason for it always bring you happiness!

"While decorating for your party, be sure to wear an elegant evening gown and plenty of sparkly jewelry. Pour yourself a refreshing glass of eggnog or a nice glass of wine and dim the lights. Then take a moment or two to admire each ornament and every strand of tinsel as you place them strategically around your lovely home. In doing so, you'll have your own private party days before the actual party begins. But more importantly, you'll find such a ritual will put you in a festive mood, a true necessity for any good hostess."

(The Complete, Total, Ultimate, Everything-You-Might-Possibly-Want-to-Know Guide to Hosting the Best Christmas Parties Ever by Carol Frost)

CHAPTER 1

"The winner of the Salesperson of the Year award for Pfunn Party Supplies Wholesale Distributors is . . . Carol Frost!" announced Festus Pfunn, the owner and CEO of our company. He was a man who could've easily doubled for Santa Claus himself, had he traded his elegant black evening-suit for one made of red velvet and trimmed with white fur. Especially since he exuded St. Nick's jolly disposition, frequently laughing in a bowl-full-of-jelly fashion.

I scooted my chair back from a round table in a sea of round tables in the hotel ballroom, all decked out with red, gold, and green Christmas decorations. Then I swished across the floor in my long, red gown, until I reached the ornately decorated podium. It was five days before Christmas, and the "ho-hum" instead of "ho-ho-ho" applause from the rest of the employees wasn't just a result of their being required to attend this holiday party and award ceremony. Nor was it because most of them would've preferred to be home with their families instead of being here, in slightly snowy Cincinnati, the company's headquarters. No, the truth was, the less than enthusiastic clapping mostly showed the complete lack of surprise that I'd won this coveted award, along with its accompanying bonus check.

Again.

To be honest, I wasn't exactly surprised myself. After all, of the twelve years that I'd been with the Pfunn company, I'd taken the trophy home ten times. While my sales throughout the year were acceptable, I always cleaned up big time when it came to holiday party paraphernalia. That's when I pushed and promoted our company's newest and shiniest Yuletide merchandise to all my clients, from major party supply chains to the Mom-and-Pop establishments in my four-state area. And since my name still meant something to so many of those store owners, they took my advice on what every well-decked-out Christmas party would be sporting this year. Then they happily signed on the dotted line and bought in triplicate. If not quadruplicate. Meaning, my holiday-time sales numbers outsparkled everyone else's.

As for why my name meant *anything* to *anyone*, well, that was all thanks to "the book." I'd written it long ago, back in the days when I used to host tons of Christmas parties, when my children were still small. And since I'd already been dubbed "Mrs. Christmas" by my neighbors, friends, and . . . well . . . nearly everyone around me, writing a book seemed like the logical next step. So I simply compiled my notes and recipes and pictures into one big manuscript and sold it to a publisher.

Who knew said book would become a best-seller? Not to mention, that my *Complete, Total, Ultimate, Everything-You-Might-Possibly-Want-to-Know Guide to Hosting the Best Christmas Parties Ever* would become the authoritative tome on Christmas party entertaining at the time? Naturally, the success of my book also meant plenty of TV and radio interviews, which only slightly extended my fifteen-minutes of fame. Back then, life was a bowl full of chocolate-covered cherries with red and green sprinkles on top. Encircled with golden garland and shiny silver stars.

Of course, that was before the incident.

After that, I never wrote another book, and I put my Christmas party hosting days behind me. And sure, while the book landed me a pretty penny, it wasn't enough to support my kids and me forever. Though thankfully, it was enough to help me land a great job so I *could* support us, by selling wholesale party supplies with Pfunn.

Not only that, but it also landed me many shiny trophies that were similar to the one I held in my hand now. I lifted this year's model up for all to see, before I leaned into the podium microphone and gave a different version of my same acceptance speech. I finished to more lackluster applause, noticing a few of the other salespeople were "ever green" with envy.

But I didn't let that dampen what little holiday spirit I had, and instead I plastered on my best I've-won-an-award smile and returned to my seat.

Once the ceremony had ended, people immediately started to file out and head home. Many of us had planes to catch, and I, for one, didn't plan to stick around much longer than necessary.

Except to chat with my friend, Sylvia, who made a beeline for my table. "Congratulations," she said with a hug. "You earned it."

As always, Sylvia took graciousness beyond the normal standards and turned it into something so artistic you could practically hang it in the Guggenheim. Especially since we'd both started working for the Pfunn company the same year, and she'd yet to win the very trophy I had sitting in front of my dessert plate. But instead of showing any kind of envy or resentment, she simply beamed with joy every single time I won. A girl couldn't ask for a more true-blue kind of friend, and should someone else ever win the annual award, I always prayed it would be her.

I also wished we could see each other more often than we did. But these days our paths only crossed at the quarterly meetings, the times when the entire sales force from around the country congregated in Cincinnati.

"Thanks," I told her as I hugged her back. "Are you all ready for your Christmas cruise?"

She slid into the chair next to mine, tugging her long chiffon skirt with her. "You'd better believe it," she said with an exaggerated nod, one that made her dark curls bounce up and down. "I am just counting the minutes. My husband is at home waiting for me, and as soon as I get there, I'm ready to go. Since that's one of the advantages of being a traveling salesperson . . ."

"Your suitcase is always packed," I finished the old adage with a laugh.

"Yup. You got it." Sylvia straightened her sequin-and-rhinestone-embellished sweater, one that featured a fully decorated Christmas tree as well as Santa in his sleigh, flying through the night sky. "We're meeting my brothers and their wives and their kids on board the ship. Plus my kids are coming. Should be a pretty big bunch. We've got a couple of suites booked, and I'm in charge of the major party on Christmas Day. So I'm taking lots of Pfunn decorations and things. I plan to 'deck the decks,' if you get my drift."

"I do. Sounds like you'll have a wonderful time." I folded an errant strand of my golden-brown hair back into my updo.

Now her tone turned sympathetic. "But how about you? Are your kids coming home for Christmas?"

I couldn't help but sigh as I continued to wrestle with my hair. "I'm afraid my son has already come home, and he appears to be staying. Since Joey graduated from college, he's been making himself quite comfortable in my basement. I don't think he ever intends to leave."

"Has he found a job yet?"

I repositioned my poinsettia and pinecone headband. "I wish. As near as I can tell, he thinks playing video games is his new career. It's going to take a major upheaval to push him out of the nest."

"Hmmm . . . Is his father helping at all?" Sylvia flagged a waiter and motioned for him to bring us both a cup of coffee.

I watched the young man place steaming cups of caffé mocha before us, complete with candy canes for swizzle sticks.

I lifted the cup to my face and breathed in the delicious aroma. "No, last I heard, he's abroad somewhere. With his new family."

Sylvia took a sip of her own coffee. "What about your daughter? Maybe you can enlist her to nudge Joseph into the real world. Will she be home for Christmas?"

"I hope so. She's got time off work and she only lives a few hours away. Though I guess her new boyfriend wants her to stay with him over the holiday. Which is sort of strange."

"Why's that?"

I shook my head. "The guy doesn't even believe in Christmas. And he certainly doesn't celebrate it."

Sylvia swirled her candy cane in her cup. "That can't be fun for Clara. I thought she loved Christmas as a little girl."

I nodded. "She did. And she still does. I'm hoping she'll figure out how wrong this guy is for her." I took a good-sized gulp of my coffee. I was going to need the caffeine if I wanted to stay awake long enough to get to the airport and onto my plane tonight.

"Would it help if you went back to hosting Christmas parties and celebrating like you used to? You know I've heard the tales of your legendary parties, and of course, I've read your book. You were the queen when it came to Christmastime entertaining. So maybe, just maybe, if you hosted one of your parties again . . ."

But I was already shaking my head. "Sorry, but no Christmas party hosting for me. Never again."

"Hmmm . . ." Sylvia murmured with a twinkle in her eyes. "You know what they say . . . 'Never say never.'"

"Nope, I'm afraid those days are over," I told her as I glanced at the clock above the podium. "A lot like this day is too, unfortunately," I added with another sigh.

Much as it would have been fun to stay and chat with my old friend, we both knew it was time to run. So we downed the rest of our coffees, hugged goodbye, and wished each other a Merry Christmas.

Then I grabbed my trophy and headed out into the hallway.

And nearly collided with Mr. Pfunn. For a moment, in the dim light, I could have sworn he really was Santa Claus. Especially when I heard his jolly old St. Nick laughter.

He beamed at me. "Congratulations again, Carol. You definitely made the 'nice list' this year. Now I trust you're headed home to be the hostess with the mostess. I can only imagine the fantastic party you've got planned."

"Um . . . well . . ." I started to say.

Funny, but nobody had actually talked about my Christmas party prowess in years. Yet tonight I'd heard about it twice in the last ten minutes.

Why? What was going on?

Normally I would have chalked it all up to being nothing but an odd coincidence. Yet tonight, my every instinct told me there was more to it than that. And I suddenly felt a strange, tingling sensation, like there was something mysterious, almost magical, in the air.

Maybe it was just the anticipation that comes with Christmas, the season for miracles.

Whatever the case, I didn't have the heart to tell Mr. Pfunn the truth, that the party-hosting part of my life was nothing but a bunch of chapters in a book that I'd closed and put on a shelf. Not when he looked so excited about the *mere* idea of me hosting a holiday soirée.

Instead, I chose to sidestep the issue by saying, "I think we'll keep it quiet this year."

His smile instantly dimmed, like someone had pulled the plug on a strand of twinkle lights. "That's a shame, Carol. I'm sure many a guest would be overjoyed to attend one of your parties."

So I had been told, all those years ago.

But that was something I didn't even want to *think* about, let alone *discuss* with my boss. So I gave him a quick peck on the cheek and wished him a Merry Christmas. Then I raced to the Concierge Desk and grabbed my luggage before I grabbed a cab. I'd allowed myself plenty of time to change out of my gown once I got to the airport, but those plans soon disintegrated along with the weather. Snow flurries filled the air and stuck to the street. Halfway to the airport, the cab came to a standstill, right smack dab in the middle of a traffic jam.

The cabbie shook his head and hit the horn. An exercise in futility, no doubt.

"Complete mismanagement of our highway system during severe weather," he said to me. "The plows should have been ready the very instant snow was spotted on the radar. A proactive approach would have produced far better results in this situation."

His words jolted me for a second. Not because of what he'd said, but because, for a moment, he'd sounded exactly like someone I knew.

Or rather, someone I used to know. My old college roommate, Kate. One who became a fortune 500 CEO, and subsequently, so rich she probably wallpapered her bedroom in Ben Franklins. She'd once been the envy of our entire graduating class.

But Kate couldn't be my cabby. It wasn't possible. Just to be sure, I leaned back and blinked a few times. But the image I saw in the rearview mirror didn't change, and I knew the scruffy-bearded man reflected back at me was a far cry from my old friend. Yet why I'd imagined for a moment that it might be her struck me as strange. Then again, I wondered why I'd even thought of her at all, on a night like tonight. So close to Christmas.

Obviously I was overtired, which had given my imagination license to work overtime. I needed a break, that much was clear, and a nice, quiet Christmas would put an end to any tricks my mind wanted to play on me. But first I needed to get to the airport, which wasn't looking terribly promising at the moment, considering the snowflakes outside my window were the size of cake-plate doilies. It was not a night fit for man nor beast, as the saying goes. And probably not a night fit for a commercial jetliner flying to Texas, either.

Now I wondered if any planes would even be taking off tonight. Which was probably a moot point, considering we were stuck in traffic and the visibility was getting worse by the second.

I sighed and sat back in my seat.

The cab driver turned and gave me a nod. "Don't you worry, my dear lady. I will get you to the airport on time. I've got a red beacon that can cut through the murkiest storm they can dish up. It'll clear the way."

With those words, he grabbed a round, red object from the passenger seat and opened his door. Cold air and snowflakes flew inside the car as he brushed snow off the roof. Then I heard a loud *thunk!* above me, and I guessed he must have put the light in place. The next thing I knew, he was back in the cab and the bright red flash from the beacon bounced off the snowflakes and the vehicles all around us.

A red flashing beacon?

As in Rudolph the Reindeer's red nose?

Or, in this case, according to the ID card attached to the back of the seat in front of me, it was "Rudolf 'Red' Dier's cab."

Seriously?

Not that I really cared *what* his name was at the moment. Mostly I just cared about the way cars started to scoot over and make room for his cab that now sported an official police-like beacon. Little by little, the cab managed to slip around and past all the vehicles in our way. Soon we were free from the rest of the mess and the snow had even started to let up. Even so, it was still slow going, since the roads were covered with snow and pretty slick.

Forty-five minutes later, he dropped me off at the terminal. It was barely enough time for me to check-in and race through the concourse. I made it to the gate just as the airline agents were closing the jetway door.

Which meant I didn't have time to change clothes.

So I strolled on board in my red dress, my skirt swiping the legs and arms of everyone sitting in an aisle seat. I braced myself for stares and snickers, as surely the other passengers would wonder why any woman in her right mind would board a plane in an evening gown.

Yet halfway to my seat — and much to my amazement — I discovered I wasn't out of place at all. Because every single person on board was dressed in Christmastime attire. In fact, I saw a virtual sea of people wearing some combination of red, green, gold, or silver. Or blue, silver, and white. Many wore lovely party dresses and nice suits, while others had donned Santa hats and antler-headbands. The variety and creativity of Christmas sweaters, with every kind of holiday scene imaginable, boggled my mind. Surprisingly, my outfit almost looked a little plain on this plane full of truly fervent Christmas fans.

My kind of people.

Or, at least, the kind of people that might have attended my Christmas parties, back in the day. Though I doubted any of them were headed to any parties now. More likely, they'd just come from some event, and thanks to the weather, they probably didn't have time to change, either. Much like me.

I located my seat near the rear of the plane and was overjoyed to find I had a row to myself. I quickly stowed my luggage and buckled myself in, right next to the window. Then finally, after a very long day, I closed my eyes and started to relax. I could hardly believe I'd made it, from the Pfunn party to the plane. What a long and harrowing journey it seemed like I'd already endured. And now, in a matter of minutes, I would be on my way home. To Austin, then north of the city, where I lived. I would celebrate Christmas with my son and my two Norwegian Forest cats, Dancer and Blitzen. And hopefully my daughter would decide to join us, too. With or without her new boyfriend.

The thought of being home with them all made me smile, and I kept on smiling when I felt the plane push back from the jetway and start to taxi out to the runway. For a moment, the plane teetered slightly, as the wind suddenly picked up. But I didn't let that faze me. I just kept my eyes closed and kept on relaxing. Without a care in the world.

That was, until the voice over the loud speaker announced, "Welcome to flight 1224, with non-stop service to the North Pole."

My eyes flew wide open, and I was just sure my heart skipped a beat or two. Did she say the North Pole? Wait a minute . . . This plane was supposed to be going to Austin! Had I gotten on the wrong plane? Or was the plane headed in the wrong direction?

What in the name of Santa Claus was going on?

Now my heart started to pound out a rumba beat in double-time, and I immediately pressed the call button for the flight attendant. Then I pulled my ticket from my purse and checked it. Sure enough, flight 1224 was supposed to be going to Austin, not to the North Pole.

Surely this was nothing but a Christmastime prank being pulled by the flight attendants. Maybe they were playing up to all the passengers dressed in Christmas attire. Or maybe most of those passengers belonged to some tour group, and the flight attendants were simply feeding into their holiday spirit by giving Santa's hometown as the plane's destination.

Laughter filled the cockpit and I noticed two flight attendants were taping garland across the overhead bins. Thankfully, a third flight attendant headed my way.

"Merry Christmas," she said with a dazzling, bright smile. "May I help you?" Her name badge read "Mindy," and she had a high, almost cartoonish voice.

"Yes," I told her, trying my best to return the smile. "I was a little concerned when you said we were headed to the North Pole. I'm supposed to be going to Austin, as you can see by my ticket." I passed my stub to her. "And I wanted to make sure there was no mistake."

Mindy crinkled her eyebrows. "I'm sorry, ma'am. But your ticket clearly shows the North Pole as your destination."

"B-b-b-u-u-u-t-t-t . . ." I started to say as I read the ticket she passed back to me. Sure enough, I saw the North Pole now printed as plain as day on my stub, when only seconds ago it had said Austin.

Suddenly I found it hard to breathe. I couldn't go to the North Pole. I had to get home. In time for Christmas. Where was the North Pole, anyway? The Artic? Alaska?

That was an awfully long trip from Cincinnati. Didn't most flights there require at least one stop to refuel?

"I'm sorry, Mindy, but I think there's been a terrible mistake . . ." I protested before I was drowned out by a voice over the intercom.

"Flight attendants, please prepare for takeoff."

"Gotta go," Mindy told me, still smiling. "I'll check back with you when we're in the air."

"Wait, I'm not supposed to be on this plane. I need to get off!"

"I'm afraid it's too late. You can't get off the plane now. We're almost to the runway." She handed me a candy cane. "Here, this will make you feel better."

And then she was gone.

I fought to get my breathing under control. How could this be happening? And for that matter, what could I do about it? Go racing down the aisle to the locked door? Throw a fit and hope they'd kick me off?

I pulled the window shade up and glanced outside. Huge snowflakes swirled furiously on the other side of the window. Now I had to wonder if the plane could even fly in this snow. Maybe I would get lucky and the flight would be grounded due to weather. It certainly wasn't an ideal scenario, but it was better than going halfway around the world to a place I didn't want to go to.

I leaned closer to the window, and over the hum of the jet engines, I thought I heard . . . sleigh bells? I also noticed an unusually large number of red strobe lights along the wings and the fuselage. What I could see of it anyway.

"All that stress will kill you," said a voice beside me. "Here, try some eggnog. You'll like it. I added a little rum to make you relax."

I turned to see someone had taken the aisle seat in my row. Someone who looked very familiar to me. In fact, she was the very woman I thought I'd seen earlier tonight, behind the wheel of my cab.

My old college roommate and best friend from those days. Kate Richards.

Under normal circumstances, I would have been overjoyed to see her.

But these were hardly normal circumstances. And there was one gigantic problem with this picture.

Kate had died in a plane crash over a year ago.

"When deciding on a guest list for your party, don't be afraid to include old friends, ones you may not have seen in years. Then make sure you address each of your beautiful party invitations by hand, using a pen with red, green, or gold ink. Sprinkle a little cinnamon and nutmeg into each envelope, so your addressees will immediately sense a party atmosphere upon opening their invitations. Meaning, they'll arrive at your house in the perfect mood for your party."

(The Complete, Total, Ultimate, Everything-You-Might-Possibly-Want-to-Know Guide to Hosting the Best Christmas Parties Ever by Carol Frost)

CHAPTER 2

For a few seconds, I could hardly breathe. A very big part of me wanted to scream.

"Kate . . . what are you doing here?" I finally managed to mutter.

She was pretty pale, but other than that, she looked as gorgeous as she always does. Or rather, *did*. Full, long dark hair and brilliant blue eyes. Nose and cheekbones that looked like they'd been sculpted. Probably because they had been, by a brilliant plastic surgeon.

"Surprised to see me?" She flashed her million-dollar smile.

"'Surprised' is a good word. For starters. 'Shocked' works well, too. 'Hallucinating' probably fits the best though."

"Is that any way to talk to an old friend?"

"How is it possible that I'm even talking to you at all? You're dead . . ." I sort of gasped. "Your private jet went down near Aspen."

She raised her brows. "Tell me about it. The whole thing's given me a real fear of flying. You have no idea how much courage it took for me to get on this plane."

"Huh? What exactly are you afraid of? You can't be any deader."

Kate shook her head. "Same old Carol. You haven't changed one bit. Always focused on the details instead of looking at the big picture."

"I'm sorry, but I watched your casket being lowered into the ground. So the fact that you're sitting here now is a detail I can't quite overlook."

"And there's your problem." Kate took a sip of her eggnog. "Rather than saying, 'Hey, Kate, good to see you again,' you're focusing in on my only flaw."

"Excuse me for noticing that you're a . . ."

"Ghost? Spirit? Specter? Do you have a problem with that? Are you discriminating against me simply because I no longer have an earthly form? Are you apparition-phobic?"

I nodded. "Yes, yes, and yes."

"Poor little Carol. You need to learn to live a little."

"That seems like very strange advice coming from a dead person."

"There you go again, harping on that whole 'dead' thing. Yeesh, you're a broken record."

I blinked a few times, wondering if my eyes were playing tricks on me again. "So what are you doing here?"

"Finally. Now we're getting somewhere. I'm here to warn you."

I choked and *thunked* a hand to my chest. "Warn me?"

"Yes," she nodded. "That's right. Like all good harbingers from the great beyond, I come with a dire warning. So here it is: Don't make the same mistake that I made."

I could hardly believe my ears. "Okay, now I know I'm hallucinating. Because you never made a single mistake in your entire life. You're Kate. Or, rather, you were Kate. You were on the fast track to success the minute you had that diploma in your hot little hands. You became the CEO of a fortune 500 company. You got so rich you didn't even know what to do with all that money. Yet here we went to the same school, got the same degree, and you ended up making gazillions while I ended up scrounging to find a job later in life. Out of desperation."

"And therein lies the monumental mistake I made. Because making money was the *only* thing I ever did. And guess what, the saying is true — you can't take it with you. Believe me, I've tried. But there's not a single bank or investment firm in the afterlife. And worst of all, there's no place to go shoe shopping."

"I'm sorry to hear that . . . but how often do you actually get to wear great shoes in the hereafter?" I asked and immediately wished I hadn't. "Not that it matters. Either way, I still don't see you as some kind of loser. You were the envy of our entire graduating class."

Kate shook her head and made a *tsk-tsk-tsking* sound. "Oh, poor Carol. All that beauty and brains but still missing the insight that matters. Listen carefully, would you? Once I became super successful, I never had time for the people in my life. I never got married, and I didn't see my friends anymore, and I never hosted another Christmas party. Do you remember our senior year, when you and I co-hosted that huge Christmas party for our sorority?"

Despite my annoyance with this specter beside me, I couldn't help but smile. "I do remember. We went all out. We bought tons of stuff at a thrift store, and we spent weeks making homemade decorations. I remember cutting out a million snowflakes from paper and hanging them everywhere."

"And we had whole teams of girls baking cookies and making cupcakes."

I glanced out the window again, at snowflakes that were almost as large as the ones we'd cut out back then. "Not to mention, trimming the tree and every door in the house. They dubbed it the Christmas party of the decade. Everyone had such a wonderful time. In fact, the last I heard, they're still talking about that party. It's become legendary. No other seniors have ever put on a party that compares to the one we hosted."

"That's right," Kate said. "And believe it or not, it was the last party I *ever* hosted."

I wasn't sure I'd heard her correctly. "What? No way. You must have hosted tons of parties after that. Maybe for work or something."

She shook her head. "Nope. Not another single one. Never, ever, ever. I couldn't be bothered. I had staff who took care of things like that for me. And those so-called parties were nothing but business events. I never put a personal stamp on a single one of them, and I never invited personal friends."

"That's a shame, because you sure knew how to throw a great party."

She furrowed her brows and pointed a bony finger at me. "You're one to talk. Little Miss 'I've Given Up on Hosting Christmas Parties' yourself. Don't bother to deny it."

I squinted my eyes. "How would you know what I've been doing? Or not doing? We lost contact years and years ago."

"Don't change the subject. I know all kinds of things. For instance, I know you used to be the queen of Christmas party planning. You were fantastic at it, and you loved at-home entertaining. But then you quit. Gave up. Ceased any and all entertaining. Went belly up when it came to holiday bashes."

I rolled my eyes. "This hallucination is starting to take a very ugly turn . . ."

"I'm telling you, Carol. You've got to listen to me before it's too late. Don't make the same mistake I made. Go back to hosting your wonderful parties again. They made tons of people happy at Christmas. They filled people with the Christmas Spirit like nothing else could. You gave people memories to last a lifetime. Just like we did at the party we hosted for our sorority."

"Yes, that's all true. And all very lovely. But I'm a different person now."

"Maybe, in some ways. But deep down, you're still the same Carol you've always been. You've got the same gifts and talents. If you wanted to, you could still decorate Christmas cookies that are worthy of their own gallery exhibit."

I lowered my eyebrows and stared at my dearly departed friend. I had to say, this was one apparition who certainly knew how to get my hackles up. Not that I'd ever had a conversation with a ghost before.

"So tell me," I said through clenched teeth, "what exactly is your game plan here? You thought you'd just show up from the dead and tell me what to do with my life?"

Her blue eyes turned stormy. "A life that you're wasting. That's why I'm here to change your mind. And mark my words, before you set foot inside your beautiful home again, you'll have a Christmas party all planned out and ready to roll."

That made me laugh. "Not on your life. Or death, as the case may be. Because I'll never host another Christmas party again. And I'm looking forward to simply going home and enjoying a very peaceful Christmas."

She responded with the stereotypical creepy laughter that every ghost in every horror movie has ever laughed, and in her case, I was pretty sure she was just doing it for effect. "Oh, I'm afraid you're not going anywhere. At least not *anywhere* you planned to go."

By now I'd had about all I could take of this strange scenario. Whatever it may be. I was pretty sure her presence was nothing more than a product of my exhausted mind. And planning a party was the last thing I would even consider at the moment, since clearly the only thing I needed to be planning was an extended beach vacation.

Much as I loved the idea of seeing my old friend one more time, I knew this whole scene wasn't real. And I decided to put an end to the bizarre optical illusion beside me by simply closing my eyes and trying to take a nap.

But the supposed specter refused to be silenced. "You can try to shut me out all you want, but it won't work. I'm not finished with you yet. Before this flight ends, you'll be visited by three more spirits. Ghost hosts, actually. The first will be the Ghost Host of Christmas Past, and the second will be the Ghost Host of Christmas Present. Then finally . . ."

I opened my eyes again. "Wait, let me guess . . . the Ghost Host of Christmas Future? Seriously? Ghost hosts?"

"Catchy, isn't it?" She smiled and downed the rest of her eggnog.

I rolled my eyes. "Kate, I know you mean well, but . . ."

"No buts about it, my old friend. You've got to heed my warning, before it's too late. Now I'd suggest you hang on tight and enjoy the ride. Because you're about to take off."

She'd barely spoken the words when I was thrust against the back of my seat as the airplane went racing and sliding down the runway. I glanced outside at the heavy snow, and wondered how the pilot would even consider taking off in such poor visibility. Especially when, judging by the way the plane was careening down the runway, it was pretty apparent we were sliding on ice.

A scream rose in my throat just before I heard a deep voice over the loud speaker. "Ladies and gentlemen, this is

Captain St. Nicholas speaking. We'll have this sleigh in the air any moment now. So sit back, have some cookies, and enjoy the jingle bells."

Jingle bells? Huh?

Was he kidding me? How was I supposed to enjoy anything at the moment, when, for all I knew, these moments might be my last? While the sound of sleigh bells grew louder outside, I looked down at my knuckles that were firmly wrapped around the ends of the armrests. I didn't think they could possibly get any whiter. Not even when the nose of the plane suddenly went up at a forty-five degree angle, and as near as I could tell, we were airborne. Amazingly, I didn't know whether I should be happy or upset. After all, as far as I knew, we were still headed to the North Pole.

I glanced over to see how Kate was holding up and, much to my surprise, her seat was now empty.

So I had just imagined the entire episode.

Still, I had to wonder why Kate had come into my mind at all tonight, and if any of what I had imagined was true. While I knew that she'd died in a plane wreck, I wondered if the part about her not hosting another Christmas party was accurate or not.

Suddenly I wished I'd made more of an effort to keep in touch with her over the years. But everything had changed the second we graduated from college. She took the fast track to business success, and I was busy planning a Christmas wedding to Daniel. Our reception was the second huge Christmas party that I had ever hosted, in what was about to become a long line of Christmas parties, each more dazzling than the last.

But that was all part of my past, and certainly held no place in my future. If only this upcoming, unplanned landing in the North Pole wasn't about to be part of my future, either. I still didn't understand how my flight plans had gotten so mixed up. Something must have happened at the airport during my rush to check in and get to my gate. Yet regardless of the reason for the error, I still had to get my flight situation straightened out. So I could get home.

By Christmas.

I reached up, ready to push my call button, until I noticed the flight attendants were now standing in the aisle and about to do their safety demonstration. But instead of raising their arms to point to the emergency exits, they led the entire plane full of passengers in a rousing round of "Jingle Bells." Like choir conductors leading a choir.

I sighed, knowing full well they'd never hear a call button over the ruckus.

In the aisle just behind my row, the unmistakable smell of roast beef wafted up to tantalize me. In fact, I was pretty sure it was actually Beef Wellington with a side of roasted asparagus that I smelled. My mouth immediately began to water. I looked up to see a very tall flight attendant reach over to pass me a plate with a cheerful, "Bon Appetite!"

I gasped and barely managed to take the plate from her. I wasn't sure if I was more surprised to find the airlines serving food — gourmet, even — or that I was staring straight into the face of Julia Child.

For a moment or two, I was speechless, until I finally managed to utter, "You're . . . you're . . . Julia Child. You're dead . . ."

To which she responded with a wave of her hand, "My heavens, no! I'm not Julia Child at all. Now please try that Beef Wellington. And make sure it's not too rare."

I cut off a small bite as instructed and watched while she did her best to squeeze into the aisle seat in my row.

"My, but they don't make these seats large enough to fit us tall girls, now do they?" she said in a lyrical voice. "Good thing I'm a ghost, or I wouldn't be able to squeeze in here at all. In my day, airline seats were made to be comfortable."

"You're a ghost . . .?"

"Well, yes. That I am. I'm the Ghost Host of Christmas Past."

"You're one of the ghost hosts? The ones I was warned about?"

"My, yes. Now eat up, because I've come to take you on a little trip back in time."

That's when I realized, if I was going to eat my meal, I was going to have to pick my chin up off the floor first . . .

Did that mean we were no longer heading for the North Pole?

"While party fads may come and go, holding fast to traditions is an important hallmark of any outstanding Christmas party. When deciding on a menu, don't forget to include the classics, such time-tested favorites as eggnog and decorated sugar cookies, or anything made with candy canes and peppermint. Remember, Christmas is a time when we return to our roots. So think of days gone by and revisit the traditions we all hold so dear."

(The Complete, Total, Ultimate, Everything-You-Might-Possibly-Want-to-Know Guide to Hosting the Best Christmas Parties Ever by Carol Frost)

CHAPTER 3

I was mid-bite and barely half finished with my Beef Wellington when the Ghost Host of Christmas Past reached for my plate and utensils. She even grabbed the fork from my hand and the napkin from my lap. But having been taught not to speak with my mouth full, I didn't protest her unusual actions.

Instead, I just watched wide-eyed as she dropped my plate and silverware into the trash bin of her flight attendant's cart. Then she scooted the cart forward, opening up the aisle next to our row. With a little maneuvering, she managed to push herself out of her seat and into the aisle, bringing all six feet plus of her body to a full-standing position.

She frowned and tapped her 1950s-style wristwatch. "Oh dear, I fear the darn thing is stuck. That means we're probably late already. So if you would please follow me, we'll get down to business."

"Follow you? Hold on a minute. I was only told I'd be *receiving* visitors. Not *going* somewhere with someone."

Especially a "someone" who wasn't even really a "somebody," but rather a specter of her former self.

"I believe I'll stay here, in my seat, thank you very much. I'm quite comfortable."

Or, at least, I was comfortable. Until a chilly wind suddenly filled the cabin and my words of protest were blown away in the breeze.

"Hurry," the ghost said, with urgency now rising in her voice. "No time to dillydally. We've got a tight schedule to keep."

"A schedule? I wasn't told about a schedule."

Frankly, the only schedule I cared about involved catching the next scheduled flight out of the North Pole so I could get home on time.

But that concern soon became the least of mine when a huge blast of air unfastened my seatbelt and lifted me up and out of my seat with what felt like a dozen icy hands. Cold chills ran a road rally up and down my spine, making me shiver violently. The next thing I knew, I was in the aisle and being tugged toward the back of the plane by this very tall ghost of a flight attendant.

To make matters worse, once we passed the partition that separated the cabin from the crew station, I noticed something was missing. Something pretty important.

Something like the left rear exit door.

I gasped and tried to pull away from this Julia Child look-alike ghost who was intent on dragging me ever closer to that opening. My heart pounded in my throat while my red gown whipped around my legs.

"All right now, here we go," the ghost host said with great cheer in her voice.

Having only three feet of airplane left between us and the dark, snowy world outside didn't seem to faze her one bit. In fact, it became very apparent that she planned to take us straight out that opening.

Silly me, while I'd certainly accessorized my red gown with plenty of Christmas finery, I'd forgotten the addition of a color-coordinated parachute.

Not that a parachute would have mattered at 35,000 feet, where the temperatures were probably so far below zero they'd reached a whole new system of measurement.

"Stop!" I yelled above the frigid wind. "I am not taking another step. And we'd better warn the crew and passengers about this!"

My ghost host stared at me in disbelief. "And ruin all their fun? My goodness gracious, they're having a wonderful party out there, though I noticed you hadn't bothered to join in. Your dear old friend, Kate, told me you had a problem. I see she wasn't exaggerating."

I tried to dig in the heels of my silver-sequined pumps and prevent this specter from propelling me forward. "I've got a problem, all right. One that involves deadly heights and life-threatening temperatures."

But it was as though I hadn't even spoken at all, because she continued to pull me ever closer toward that exit. Obviously, the situation didn't bother her in the least. Then again, that was likely a big difference between being dead or alive. Dead people probably didn't get too worked up about perilous predicaments. Whereas I, on the other hand, was about to die from fright alone.

Especially when the ghost host had the audacity to smile at me before she said, "Time to put on your party face."

Then a mere nanosecond later, the plane banked sharply to the right and the ghost and I went tumbling, tumbling,

tumbling out into the night. My scream was lost in the pelting snowflakes and I could barely breathe as the wind pushed against me as we fell, with my dress practically turning into a giant kite.

"Don't stay out too long, or you'll get frostbite!" another voice yelled.

Frostbite? Frostbite was a given. And it was way down on my list of things to worry about at the moment, coming in long after such items as freezing to death or getting smooshed when I hit the frozen ground.

But wait a minute . . . I recognized that sweet voice. It certainly wasn't the voice of the Ghost Host of Christmas Past. Suddenly the world around me began to lighten, and the snow started to let up. I caught a glimpse of a beautiful red, wool coat only seconds before I landed in a snow drift, as softly as a feather landing atop a pillow.

The ghost host was already on her feet beside me, and she helped me to mine. That's when I noticed a little girl wearing the exact same coat that I'd worn when I was nine years old. My mother had bought it for me before Christmas that year, saying I'd want to look nice to go Christmas caroling.

"Hello, little girl," I called out.

But she didn't seem to notice me and kept right on building a snowman.

"She can't see or hear you," the ghost told me. "But look closer. Do you recognize that child? Do you remember that house?"

And all at once, I did. In fact, that little girl looked a lot like . . . me. When I was that age.

"Is that . . .?" I started to ask.

"Yes, it's you. You were nine and staying at your grandmother's house for the day."

That's when I knew whose voice had warned me about getting frostbite. Joy leapt in my heart. It was my beloved grandmother I'd heard.

And it was my grandmother who opened the back door and glanced outside. "Carol, would you like to come help me decorate these cookies?"

"Grams," I murmured as tears slid down my cheeks. "I didn't think I'd ever see her again. I loved her so much."

"Yes, I know," the ghost host said with a nod. "Your grandmother taught you lots about hosting Christmas parties."

"She did? I don't remember that."

"Ah, but come inside and take a look."

Seconds later we floated into my grandmother's kitchen, where it was bright and warm, and the aroma of cookies baking filled the air. There sat me as a child, helping my grandmother decorate some absolutely stunning sugar cookies. We were both wearing our aprons, and my hair was tied back in a ponytail.

"Each cookie should be a work of art, Carol," my Grams instructed little girl me. "They'll be at the heart of our Christmas party."

Then she showed me how to mix the glaze and add the proper amounts of food coloring to create just the right colors. We dipped the cookies in the glaze and set them on wax paper to dry. After that, I watched as she taught me how to work a piping bag, holding her hands over mine as we squeezed the icing onto the cookies to decorate them even more. Then we added sprinkles and sparkles, and before long, our cookies went from frumpy to fantastic. Each one was a little masterpiece of its own.

"This is so much fun," my nine-year-old self told my Grams.

She nodded with a smile. "Yes, it is fun. But more important than that, we're doing something extra special for our guests, to bring them joy at Christmas."

"We are?"

"Yes," my Grams said in her warm voice. "You must remember, Carol, that Christmas is all about giving. And not about what presents we're going to get. Hosting a wonderful Christmas party is one of the best gifts you can give to others, since you can truly make people happy."

"Oh, I get it. That sounds very nice, Grams."

To which my grandmother had simply smiled before she pulled another batch of cookies from the oven.

We had just finished decorating the cookies when the doorbell rang. My Grams and my young self both wiped our hands on our aprons, and rushed to answer the door. My ghost host and I followed.

Outside on the front porch were two of my grandmother's friends, Laurel and Betty. Judging by the redness of their noses, I had a good idea they had walked the entire way.

"Come in, come in," my Grams insisted. "Don't stand out there in the cold."

Laurel had a very lyrical laugh. "We're sorry to drop in on you like this, Mary. But Betty called earlier and she got her pictures back from her vacation."

"And I just had to show them to you," Betty added.

My grandmother took their coats. "Carol, can you collect their gloves and scarves?"

"Sure, Grams," young me said, doing my best to sound grown-up.

"We'll hang them in the hall closet while I put the kettle on to boil," Grams told me.

Betty handed me her mittens and a plaid scarf. "My goodness, Carol, I can't believe how much you've grown."

"I'm almost ten," I informed her.

Laurel's eyes went wide. "You're such a big girl. And obviously a very good helper."

Grams beamed at me. "Yes, she is. She's been over here helping me bake all day."

"Lovely," Laurel replied as she handed me her own scarf and gloves. "So that's why it smells so good in here."

"And you'll be the first to sample our Christmas cookies," Grams said, sounding very pleased. "Why don't you two ladies take a seat here in the living room, and Carol and I will bring out tea and cookies."

Grown-up me turned to my ghost host. "Wait just a minute . . . did these ladies even call to say they'd be coming over? It looks like they stopped by with no warning at all."

The ghost host shook her head. "Back in those days, people simply dropped in for a visit. It wasn't unusual at all. And a good hostess always prepared tea or coffee. As well as provided a delicious snack.

We continued to watch as my little girl self followed Grams to the hall closet, where we put the coats and things away.

"But Grams," the child me said with panic in her voice. "Aren't those cookies supposed to be for the party?"

My Grams smiled at me. "Don't you know, Carol? We made extras, so we'd have something just in case someone dropped by. These ladies are our guests, and it's important that we make them feel at home. Now, I'll send you out with the tea tray full of things, while I brew up a pot of tea."

Minutes later, there was little girl me, carrying a tray loaded with pink china cups and saucers, along with a creamer filled with real cream, and a sugar bowl stacked with sugar cubes. Spoons and cloth napkins were on one side, while a plate full of our newly created sugar cookies was on the other.

Not long after that, my Grams brought in a matching pink teapot full of tea, using her favorite potholder to help her carry it.

Then the specter and I watched as young me enjoyed a perfect cup of tea, filled with cream and two sugars, while listening to the ladies talk about everything under the sun. The cookies, of course, brought exclamations of pure wonderment.

And grown-up me watched the whole thing. It had been such a lovely, relaxed afternoon, and now I realized how much

I had learned that day about entertaining guests, even on a very small scale.

Until the icy fingers of my ghost host touched my shoulder, jolting me out of the moment. "We need to move on," she informed me like a tour guide keeping a group on course.

"But I don't want to leave yet. It's so warm and happy here. And I want to see my grandmother a little while longer."

Unfortunately, the ghost beside me was unrelenting. "I'm afraid we're on a very tight schedule."

"Schedule?" I repeated as she hauled me from the room and floated us back out into the cold.

I shivered in the winter chill, aching to return to the warmth of my grandmother's living room.

But seconds later, I suddenly found myself at another Christmas party, this time an evening event full of people. And from what I could tell, the party was sensational. The house lights were dimmed while strands of twinkle lights glowed from trees and across the crown molding and elsewhere. The presentation of the food was a true exercise in artistry, and the perfectly placed decorations glimmered in the warm light. Bing Crosby crooned from carefully placed speakers, as the guests all laughed and chatted, clearly having the time of their lives.

I had to say, I couldn't have been more impressed. Whoever was hosting this party had done so with amazing skill. As I glanced around the room, I found myself smiling more and more. I realized I had entered the home of a truly outstanding hostess, one who had gone to great lengths to give her guests an absolutely enjoyable evening.

And then everything suddenly looked familiar and I remembered that I'd seen this party before. In fact, it was a Christmas party that I had hosted, in my own home. Years and years ago.

And that's when my stomach practically sank to my knees. Especially when I realized exactly which party this had been.

The last Christmas party I had ever hosted.

Which meant it was also the night of "the incident." The night when my life changed and was never the same again.

"Good conversation is an important aspect of any party. As a hostess, it's your job to go from one small cluster of people to the next, subtly dropping snippets of information here and there, to start conversations along the way. Be sure to introduce your guests to one another and dispense some interesting tidbit about each one. In other words, do your best to make your guests comfortable, as though your home were their home."

(The Complete, Total, Ultimate, Everything-You-Might-Possibly-Want-to-Know Guide to Hosting the Best Christmas Parties Ever by Carol Frost)

CHAPTER 4

"I am not staying," I informed the Ghost Host of Christmas Past. "It's absolutely cruel that you even brought me here."

"My heavens, not at all," she said with a smile. "I should imagine anyone would want to be here. This is a superb party."

I crossed my arms. "Yes, it is, and I remember it well. Because I was there, hosting it. It was the perfect party. At least, it started out that way."

The ghost host put a hand to her chest and sighed. "My, yes, it is a vision of hosting splendor. Look at this ambience. It's as though the party guests have been transported to another world. The tinsel and ornaments hung across the rooms are simply divine, creating space and warmth all at once. Then there's the music, some of my favorite Christmas classics mixed with new songs. I couldn't have done it better myself."

"But it all went wrong," I murmured.

"And it was the last party you ever hosted," she said with a nod.

I glanced at the curved staircase. "If only I'd never gone up those stairs."

The ghost host shook her head. "You had to know the truth. And now you need to *deal* with that truth. Time for you to go back up those stairs again."

"Again?" I sputtered. "I refuse. Why on earth would I put myself through that a second time? I won't do it."

"But you must. To go on with the future, you must face the past and then let it go."

"Speaking of going, I believe it's time that I was going. Now do that floating thing you do and get me out of here."

And sure enough, we started to float, all right. But instead of being taken out the door, I felt myself being moved up the stairs, completely against my will. I watched helplessly as I passed chasing twinkle lights and garland wrapped around the banister. With silver, glitter-covered stars hanging between the spindles. In any other setting, I would have been mesmerized by it all. Delighted.

But not tonight. Not on this night.

"Please, I'm begging you," I told the ghost. "Don't make me go up there."

I stared at her now steely, pale face, and at her cold, unfeeling eyes. How could she do this to me? Once in my life had been enough. Did I really need to relive this?

We finally reached the top of the stairs and went down the back hallway. The door to the room at the end of the hall had been closed and now magically creaked open as the ghost moved me forward. Ever closer.

To the guest room, the place where everyone's coats had been laid on the bed. But once we got there, I could see in the dim light that the coats weren't the only thing lying on the bed.

"We shouldn't be doing this," my husband murmured into the ear of Sally, my neighbor and best friend at the time.

Or so I had thought.

Sally giggled and rolled on top of him, the sequins of her slinky evening gown flashing even in the dim light. "She'll never know. She's busy downstairs, hosting the ultimate Christmas party."

"It's too risky," Daniel had argued, as he ran his fingers through her blonde curls and kissed her neck. "We might get caught."

And seconds later, they were, when my younger self had entered the room, as I brought up the coat of a late arrival. Sally's husband, Steve, had followed me, wondering if I might know where his wife had gone.

Apparently, his question had now been answered.

Then as I stood there, heartbroken and frozen in grief, Sally's husband wasted no time in going after Daniel. The blowup that followed was huge, like a scene out of a soap opera that was worthy of a daytime Emmy. My black-haired, blue-eyed husband ended up with a bloody nose and a black eye, mere minutes before he and Sally raced from the room and left the house together via the back door. Yet all the while, my guests downstairs hadn't even heard the brawl above, since the sounds of the party below had completely drowned it out.

Meaning, they had no idea what was going on.

Not until the police showed up, after Daniel amazingly decided to press charges against Sally's husband. Fighting back tears, I had the horrible task of taking the officers upstairs, where a sobbing Steve had dropped onto the bed. He was led away in handcuffs, which sent a shock wave of murmurs and gasps throughout what was left of my party. In the meantime, it took every ounce of control I could muster not to break down and bawl like a baby myself, as my confused and stunned guests quietly left my house in a hurry.

And I was left alone.

With no one to turn to, since the people in my life that I normally would have leaned on — namely my husband and my best friend — were no longer an option.

Later, when Daniel came home and packed, I learned the affair had been going on for a while. But that was all I learned, since he and Sally immediately took off for parts unknown, and I was left to explain something to my kids that I couldn't even explain myself.

Now as I watched the whole scene all over again, helplessly, the stabbing pain in my chest felt just as real now as it had back then.

That night was supposed to be the night of my greatest triumph. I had just returned from a whirlwind book tour and my book had hit the best-seller list. Besides that, my Christmas party that evening had included my publisher and my agent, and some of my oldest and dearest friends.

Yet Daniel had cruelly chosen that night to ruin it all for me.

Tears rolled down my cheeks and I turned to my ghost host. "Are you happy now? You've succeeded in making me cry. You've brought back the same pain I felt that night."

She simply raised her eyebrows. "Our most agonizing moments can turn into our greatest triumphs."

I snickered. "Are you kidding me? There was no triumph that night. I never, ever hosted another Christmas party again. And I never wrote another book."

"Quite true, all in all. But remember, that was your choice."

I gasped. While I knew you weren't supposed to speak ill of the dead, I didn't think that precluded speaking ill directly to a dead person, aka a ghost. "How can you say something so horrible? That night destroyed me."

The ghost shook her head. "It most certainly was awful. And you grieved horribly over it. But let's face it, the man was a louse."

For a moment, I was too stunned to speak.

But my ghost host didn't seem to be at a loss for words. "Yes, that's right. Daniel was a self-centered man who resented your talents, especially when he saw you at the top of your game. Look at that sensational party you hosted. Look at the way your book rose to the top of the list. But he never supported you. He was jealous and threatened by your success. And he lashed out at you in the worst way possible — by having an affair with your best friend, and setting himself up to be 'discovered,' as it were, on the night of your party. Because let's face it — it was no coincidence that he chose to have his little liaison that night in the very room where you'd be bringing your guests' coats. No, the rat wanted to be caught. And in doing so, he ruined the party that was the highlight of your career."

I wiped my tears away. "Fine. I get it. I'm better off without him."

"One would think. But in your case, you weren't. Because, after he left, you quit doing all the things you loved. You quit baking and decorating and hosting your parties. And you didn't write a second book, to follow up your first one that was fabulously successful. So even though the scoundrel took off, you still let him be a very big part of your life. He's been hurting you all these many years later, just as much as he hurt you that night."

Her words stung me to the core. "That's it!" I hollered and stomped my foot. "I've had about as much of this as I can take."

I flailed my arms, trying to fight my way out of there. And out of the whole scene.

I was still flailing my arms when I felt someone shaking my shoulder.

I woke up in my airline seat, with a real, live flight attendant leaning over me. Though it was a little hard to tell she was part of the crew, considering she wore a gold garland like a boa, and she had tiny green and red jingle bells hanging from her pillbox hat. Christmas balls dangled from her earlobes.

"You were having quite a nightmare," she told me.

I sighed, and relief coursed through my veins. So it really had been nothing but a dream after all. Everything. From the announcement over the loud speaker that said we were going to the North Pole, to seeing Kate, to my little "excursion" with the so-called Ghost Host of Christmas Past.

And what a bizarre dream it had been.

The flight attendant smiled and handed me a cup of hot chocolate. "Here, drink this. It'll make you feel better. Would you like some whipped cream on top?"

"I'd love some," I told her, feeling instantly revived.

She held a canister over my cup and squirted a nice little mound on top. She finished it off with some chocolate shavings.

"There. You'll be better in a jiff. Especially when you hear the good news. We'll be landing in the North Pole in time to see Santa take off."

"What?!" I sputtered through hot chocolate and whipped cream. "But I'm supposed to be going to Austin!"

My words were a complete waste of breath, since a few of the Christmas partying passengers had already shouted for the flight attendant, and she was halfway down the aisle to take care of them in a matter of seconds. Long before my protests had a chance to reach her ears.

And someone else plopped into the aisle seat in my row. A plump, petite woman who wasn't even five feet tall. She was dressed in what was possibly the gaudiest Christmas sweater I had ever seen. She wore a wreath of flashing twinkle lights, and a green felt circle skirt embellished with appliquéd

Christmas trees. To complete her ensemble, she had on candy-cane striped leggings and red cowboy boots.

"Buckle up, sister," she drawled in an accent more Southern than my own. "Because we're about to go on a wild ride! Nice to meet you, by the way. I'm the Ghost Host of Christmas Present."

I rolled my eyes. To think, for a moment or two, I had thought this was nothing but a dream. Instead, I now realized this entire trip was nothing but a living, breathing nightmare.

"A well-run Christmas party is like a well-oiled machine. As the hostess, remember, you are the driver of the event, much like the engineer of a locomotive. So make sure you're the one in charge, or the train might just go off the track. Don't allow your party to become a train wreck by letting a guest hijack it. And while the purpose of your party is to provide an exciting ride for your guests, don't put the brakes on the accolades. After all, you, my dear hostess, have earned them."

(The Complete, Total, Ultimate, Everything-You-Might-Possibly-Want-to-Know Guide to Hosting the Best Christmas Parties Ever by Carol Frost)

CHAPTER 5

I took a sip of my hot chocolate and stared at this newest ghost host. "I'm sorry, but I've had my fill of apparitions for one night. And believe me, I don't need any more drama like I had with that other ghost. So please go find some other poor woman to torture, thank you."

She offered me an oversized grin, with huge white teeth that momentarily flashed like fangs. "No can do, sugar pie. Because we've got some parties to attend."

"I'm not interested."

"So I've heard. But it's just not right that you quit hosting your swell Christmas parties. You've gotta get back in the saddle."

"Excuse me? I don't think so. It's a free country and my party hosting days are long gone."

"Woo-wee, baby girl! Aren't you just as stubborn as an old mule! Don't worry, I've worked with tougher cookies than you," she exclaimed, just as she handed me a beautifully iced sugar cookie, one made in the shape of a holly leaf. "Here, try this."

I rolled my eyes and decided to indulge her. I took a tiny bite from one edge, and immediately wished I hadn't. "Yeeoowch! I think I just chipped a tooth. These things are like cement."

"I told you! Tough cookies. Now let's get you to the ladies room. Looks like you're bleeding."

"Bleeding?" I put my hand to my mouth.

She jumped up and I scooted over and followed her. All the while I kept my hand to my face. She moved faster than anyone I've ever seen, and I raced to keep up with her.

She beat me to the lavatory and held the door open for me. "Here you go, little darlin'. Let's get you some tissues and get you cleaned up."

But the very second I stepped inside, I saw that I'd been duped. Because instead of finding a tight-fitting airplane bathroom, I walked into an empty room about the size of my huge walk-in closet at home. It was dimly lit, though I couldn't tell for sure where the light was coming from. Huge clouds floated across the floor.

Behind me, the ghost host was laughing. "Ha, ha! Tricked you!"

"You are not funny."

"But isn't this fun?"

"No."

"You used to throw parties that were fun, once upon a time. You made people feel happier than a June bug on a tomato plant. It was a real treat to get invited to one of your shindigs. You turned frowns upside down, little missy, for days and days afterward. You helped plenty of people feel the Christmas Spirit."

I shook my head and rolled my eyes. "Ancient history."

"Haven't you ever read the Bible, darlin'? Hebrews 13:2. 'Do not forget to entertain strangers, for by so doing some people have entertained angels without knowing it.'"

"It's not the angels that I'm worried about. Do you have any idea what happened at the last Christmas party I ever hosted?"

She was already nodding her head up and down. "I sure do, sugar pie. I also know you let your heart get frosted over. But not in a good way, not like you used to frost your Christmas cookies. So now all we gotta do is thaw out that frozen heart of yours."

With those words, she pulled another one of her Christmas cookies out of thin air. This one was in the shape of an angel and frosted with white, yellow, and blue icing.

I couldn't believe she had the nerve to try this stunt again. "I'm not falling for that. I'm going back to my seat. Wherever it is." I turned to walk out the door, but it was suddenly gone.

"There's a little problem with that idea. Because I'm not taking no for an answer. C'mon. Buck up and take a bite. I promise this one will be de-li-cious." She broke the cookie in half, to show me it really was soft on the inside.

Just to appease this very determined woman, I took a small bite. A very, very careful bite.

This time, the cookie was warm, flavorful, full of spice and the joy and happiness that only Christmas can bring. All around me, I heard laughter and felt a sense of mystery and excitement, something I hadn't felt in a long, long time.

Warm sea air blew threw my hair, and threatened to dislodge my updo once and for all. That's when I realized I was standing on the deck of a cruise ship. Oddly enough, I wasn't out of place in my long gown, since apparently it was formal night on board. All the passengers were wearing gowns and tuxedoes.

"Where are we? And why are we here?"

"You'll see," the ghost said with another one of her huge grins.

"Don't tell me you're going to trick me again." I'd barely gotten the words out when I spotted my friend, Sylvia, walking our way. She was with a huge group of people, all dressed to the nines. Their laughter and conversation filled the air as they moved closer.

"Sylvia!" I called out. "Boy, am I glad to see you. I have been having the strangest nightmare."

But my friend didn't even notice me.

The Ghost Host of Christmas Present moved to my side, with the top of her head not even reaching my shoulder. "She can't hear you. And she can't see you, either."

I sighed. "Right. I know the drill. Will we be floating along again?"

"You're right as rain, sugar. A floatin' we will go, right after I do this do-si-do!" she said before she folded her arms and did a quick dance step.

And sure enough, my new specter guide and I then floated along behind Sylvia and her group. We followed as the whole rambunctious bunch went inside and headed down a hallway. And when everyone entered the double doors of the largest suite on the ship, the Penthouse Suite, we went in, too. Only it didn't look like any ship's suite that I'd ever seen. Instead it seemed as though we'd stepped right into a Christmas wonderland, one that I knew Sylvia must have created herself. Twinkle lights were strung from one end of the room to the other, and lighted, pull-up trees were everywhere. Metallic garland and Christmas ornaments added to the ambience. Clearly, she had put the very latest from Pfunn Party Supplies Christmas party line on full display, and I had to say, it was utterly spectacular.

A few of the younger members of the group let out squeals, while some of the grownups gasped. Laughter and cheerful exclamations immediately filled the room.

"Aunt Sylvia, this is stunning!"

"It's gorgeous, Sylvia. You have truly outdone yourself."

And my dear friend, in her long emerald gown, smiled and glowed as brightly as any of the lights.

A man who must have been her brother grabbed a wineglass and raised it in the air. "To Sylvia!"

Seconds later, everyone else followed suit. Even the children raised water glasses in salute. The words, "To Sylvia!" echoed through the room.

My friend smiled and raised her own glass in the air, asking for everyone's attention. At once a hush fell over the room.

"I wish I could take credit for it all, but I must give credit where credit is due," Sylvia announced as she glanced from one face to the next. "Because, the truth is, I learned everything I know about hosting a great Christmas party from a friend of mine. Carol Frost. Not only did I read her book, but I'd heard stories about the famous parties she'd hosted. Without her, I wouldn't have had a clue how to do all this. I wish she was with us tonight, but she's not. In any case, I'd like to raise a glass to her, my dear friend. Here's to Carol!"

Whereby everyone immediately chimed in and saluted me. "To Carol!"

My chin practically fell to the floor, and I put my hand to my chest. "But I am here," I whispered. "I heard the whole thing. I can't believe what just happened . . ." Hot tears started to roll down my cheeks.

"But it *did* happen, darlin'," the ghost host whispered into my ear. "And it's just the kind of warmth we need to thaw out that frozen heart of yours."

"Why are you doing this to me?" I asked as I wiped away more and more tears. "Why did you bring me here?"

"Because, little missy, you may have tried to sweep your old life under the carpet, ever since that man done you wrong. But when you swept all the bad stuff away, you swept all the good stuff away, too. And that's a cryin' shame, considering you brought a lot of happiness to a lot of folks, and you'd best not forget it."

For the first time since I'd been thrust into this crazy altered world by these strange spirit guides, I felt a smile cross my face. I had to say, it felt good to know that I'd made a difference in someone's life. Or in the lives of so many, as this apparition had mentioned.

Now the ghost host's face broke out into another huge grin. "Whoa, golly, what's that I see? Is that frown starting to turn upside down?"

I crinkled my brows at her, but she didn't stop grinning.

And she kept on grinning when she handed me another cookie. "Here you go, darlin'. You look like you could use a pick-me-up."

"Is this another trick?"

She placed the decorated sugar cookie in my hand, and I inspected it carefully. It had been dipped in a glaze that was precisely the same combination of blue and green food coloring that I always used. And the icing piped on top was in a pattern that I had designed. Now I took a good sniff of the cookie, and immediately picked up on the scent of fresh vanilla beans, an ingredient that I always added, instead of using the cheap store vanilla that came in a bottle.

Finally, I took a bite of the cookie, and right away, I knew this beautifully decorated cookie . . .

Was one of mine.

But how could that be? I hadn't baked cookies like these in eons. And I certainly didn't have any plans to host a Christmas party of my own, an event that would have required me to bake pans and pans of my special ornately iced cookies.

I looked directly at the ghost host. "Wait a minute . . . where did you get this cookie? It's exactly like the cookies I used to bake and decorate."

"Ha! Ha! Tricked you!" she said with great mirth, as I suddenly noticed we were now standing inside a completely different party.

A party that looked an awful lot like a party that I might have once hosted. From the handcrafted snowflakes covered in Austrian crystals, to the holly, poinsettia, and white lily streamers dangling from the doorways, the decorations and the food and the lighting were clones of the illustrations and photographs that I'd included in my book. In fact, this entire party was an exact replica of the things I'd written about.

Had the ghost host transported me to another one of my own parties? Yet while I recognized things from the pages of my book, the setting didn't look the least bit familiar. And I didn't recognize a single one of the guests.

Maybe one of my readers had used my ideas to host her own party. The thought of it made me smile.

"Where are we?" I asked the ghost. "This looks exactly like one of my parties. And everyone seems to be having a wonderful time."

The ghost smiled. "It's one humdinger of a party, all right."

Then she pointed to the back of the room, where a red-haired woman in a red velvet dress was standing on a small stage, being interviewed by a television reporter.

The woman smiled in the light cast by the camera. "And you can find all my party tips, just as soon as I publish my book. After all, they don't call me Gayle 'The Great Party' Guru for nothing!"

I gasped and put my hands on my hips. "She stole my stuff! None of this is her original work. Everything here is straight out of my book. But she's taking credit for it, and claiming the ideas are her own."

The ghost host raised her eyebrows. "That girl's a horse thief, all right. She took all your ideas, didn't she? And if she publishes "her" book . . .

"Which is basically my book. But if she puts her name on it, then she's . . . she's . . . she's . . ."

"Lower than a rattlesnake at the bottom of a canyon. It's plagiarism, pure and simple."

"So why hasn't anyone noticed? Why isn't anyone saying a thing? The news reporter should be asking her about this."

The ghost host shook her head. "I hate to say it, darlin', but I think they've forgotten all about your book. It's been a long, long time since you wrote it. And you never wrote a second book to follow the first one. Plus, let's face it, you haven't hosted a party since, well, you know when . . ."

"But I had to quit all that and find a job. To feed me and my family after Daniel took off. I had no choice."

"Are you sure about that, baby girl? Did you really have to quit, or did you just give up and run away? I mean, sure, you're darn good at your job and you make a fine living, but is it really what you want to be doing? Is it your dream? The reason the good Lord put you on this planet?"

For a moment or two, I just stood there sort of sputtering. I searched the farthest recesses of my mind, but for the life of me, I couldn't come up with a catchy comeback.

Finally, I said, "Well, one thing's for sure. That little crook on that stage isn't going to get away with stealing my stuff."

My ghost host grinned. "Now that's the little spitfire everyone used to know."

I put my hands on my hips. "Take me back, spirit. Right now."

"Whatever you say, little missy. Here, have a cookie," she said with a nod and a grin, while she handed me a gingerbread man.

This time I took a big bite from the cookie, and the very second I did, I was back in my seat on the plane. And the Ghost Host of Christmas Present was gone.

For a moment, I wondered if I had imagined it all.

That was, until I looked at the gingerbread man in my hand and knew that I hadn't.

But two seconds later, I could no longer see that cookie, because the lights flickered and suddenly went out. Outside, I could see snow pelting the plane, right before it took a very definite nosedive. Yet while I screamed at the top of my lungs, I was completely drowned out by the roar of the engine. Much to my amazement, lightning suddenly shot through the plane, and that's when I noticed the aisle seat in my row was now occupied by a very large, hooded being with a scythe.

How someone had managed to get a scythe through TSA screening and then onto a plane, I could not even imagine.

Not that it mattered, because this was one plane that was headed straight for the ground. In a hurry.

"In the days leading up to your party, it's important to sit back and close your eyes for a moment, then picture your party in your mind's eye, almost like you're gazing into a crystal ball. See yourself in your stunning attire, with jewelry that outshines even your brightest decorations. Imagine yourself gliding from guest to guest, engaging in witty repartee, bringing oodles of laughter from all around you, for wherever you walk, you'll spread joy like a fairy godmother scatters glitter."

(The Complete, Total, Ultimate, Everything-You-Might-Possibly-Want-to-Know Guide to Hosting the Best Christmas Parties Ever by Carol Frost)

CHAPTER 6

I could hardly believe my eyes or ears. Here I was, thrust so hard against the back of my seat that I felt I might actually become fused to it, thanks to the force of the plane shooting straight toward the ground. Yet oddly enough, the passengers in the rest of the cabin were now singing, "We Wish You a Merry Christmas," at the top of their lungs, as though they had no earthly idea that we were about to crash. To make things worse, I now recognized the creature sitting in my row, one who was seemingly undisturbed and hadn't bothered with a seatbelt, a creature whose breaths came out in puffs of smoke.

The Grim Reaper.

As a general rule, I tend to consider things like plummeting planes with the Specter of Death on board as being pretty high on my list of things to avoid in life. And if I had ever complained about a flight before — maybe because of the lack of legroom, or someone reclining a seat, or such — it didn't even begin to compare to this. Those problems all seemed like a mint-peppermint-cream-frosted cakewalk now.

Especially when the specter pointed one of his bony fingers at me. That's when I noticed that he, or it, absolutely reeked of cinnamon and nutmeg.

And while I'm certainly a fan of both those fine spices, "overuse of a spice can be overpowering. If not a culinary crime," I had written in my own book.

I hated the idea of spending my very last moments of this life sitting next to a passenger who had committed such an olfactory faux pas.

Thankfully, I didn't have to worry about that when, seconds later, the plane leveled off and seemed to slide on its belly, like a sled skimming across a snowy plain, until it came to a halt, whereby whole sections of the cockpit broke away. Soft snow, as white as powdered sugar, fluttered freely into what was left of the plane. Above us, handfuls and handfuls of brilliant stars sparkled in the midnight-blue sky, like rows and rows of Christmas twinkle lights hung in the heavens.

But they weren't as bright as the glowing red eyes under the specter's hooded robe.

It was enough to make me roll my own eyes. "You don't get any points for originality, that's for sure," I told him. "Let me guess . . . you're the Ghost Host of Christmas Future."

The creature responded with a very slow nod, before pointing to the aisle. As near as I could tell, I was supposed to follow him.

"Fine," I said. "Let's get this over with. So I can get on with my life."

The ghost led the way toward the back of the plane without saying a word. Apparently, he was the strong-smelling, silent type.

As I gathered my skirts and tagged along behind him, I noticed a snowball fight had broken out amongst the other passengers, who had mysteriously managed to don hats and mittens and scarves. A bunch of people at the front of the plane were busy decorating a brightly lit Christmas tree that had sprung up from out of nowhere.

The ghost pulled up a trapdoor in the floor of the plane and held it for me.

"How very kind of you," I said with sarcasm dripping on my every word.

I moved down a flight of stairs, my skirts swishing along behind me, into a dark, cold room whose only light came from an old television set. It appeared I had walked into someone's living room. A very sparsely decorated living room, at that.

There was a picture on the wall of a perfectly decked out Christmas tree, yet the only actual tree in the room was about a foot high, covered with a tiny strand of garland and a few ornaments. It had been placed on an end table next to a wingback chair.

A very old woman sat in that chair, watching "A Charlie Brown Christmas." She laughed along with every quip and cute comment from the Peanuts® characters. On the woman's lap was a large Himalayan cat with a red bowtie collar.

The woman was dressed in a wrinkled red evening gown, one that appeared to be an older version of the very gown I had on now, had it been stuffed in the back of a closet for years and years.

I gasped and turned to the tall ghost who now stood behind the chair. "Can she hear me, spirit?"

He shook his head no.

"Is that . . . is that me? In my golden years?"

To which he merely nodded.

I watched the woman a little longer, until she picked up a single Christmas cookie from a plate on the end table.

"Well, Clarence," she said with a warble in her voice. "Looks like it's just you and me at this Christmas party."

She held her cookie in the air, as though toasting some unknown person. "You know, Clarence, I used to host Christmas parties. Lots of them. Some said I was the best."

To which the cat merely responded with a flick of his tail.

"Here's to us," she said before she took a bite of the cookie.

I *thunked* my hand to my chest. "Where are my kids, and my grandkids? Why am I all alone? Why am I not sitting with a bunch of people, at some Christmas party that my daughter or granddaughter might be hosting?"

But the ghost host just shook his head.

"Say something, would you, please?"

Again, the big oaf just kept his big trap shut.

And that was about all I could take. After all, we were at a party of sorts, albeit a small one. And there's just nothing ruder than a guest who won't speak when spoken to. Or won't even bother to try to join in on the conversation.

I put my hands on my hips. "All right, mister, I've had just about as much of this bad behavior as I can take. You are really getting on my nerves."

I wasn't sure, but I could have sworn I heard the ghost start to choke.

But I wasn't finished with him yet, in fact, I was just getting warmed up. "I know you're acting all scary and sinister, and I'm supposed to be frightened of you, but I'm not. As for you, the least you could do is have some good manners and answer me while you're taking me along on this journey. Or whatever you might call it."

And that's when the giant-sized so-called Grim Reaper started to laugh. Like he was enjoying the whole thing.

I instantly gave him a death stare of my own. "That's about enough of that. This whole big, dark, and imposing act isn't going to work on me. In my business, we have a name for people . . . or creatures . . . like you! We call you the 'Party Killers.' You're the worst kind of party guest imaginable. You show up at someone's home after they've worked hard to set the stage and host the perfect party, and you do everything you can to ruin it. You brood, you mope, and you criticize. As far as I'm concerned, you can just leave me alone."

To which the specter held out his hand to shake.

What was this? An apology?

Well, if he wanted to be the "bigger" person, or the bigger "being," as it were, well, then I was big enough to forgive him.

"Apology accepted," I said with a smile as I took his hand.

Only to receive an immediate shock in my palm.

From a joy buzzer.

"*Yeeoow!*" I screamed before I pulled back. "Hey, what was that for? That was a lousy thing to do." For emphasis, I kicked him in what I thought was the vicinity of his knee.

He hollered and folded like a lawn chair. "Okay, okay, lady. I get the picture. Give me a break, would you?"

So . . . the spirit could speak after all.

"Who are you?" I asked him. "And what's with the Grim Reaper routine?"

The next thing I knew, the so-called Specter of Death pulled off his huge oversized hooded robe and removed a mask with fake red eyes.

Underneath his costume he appeared to be a thirty-year-old with a mop of curly, brown hair and a very scraggly beard. He was wearing a crumpled 1960s plaid suit jacket over a stained t-shirt, and his saggy blue jeans looked like they hadn't seen the inside of a washing machine. Ever. Then there was that overpowering smell of cinnamon and nutmeg. Which I soon guessed was some kind of cologne to cover up his aversion to bathing.

While he may not have been the Grim Reaper, he was still a good hostess' worst nightmare, a true party killer. His lack of hygiene alone could have cleared out any room, not to mention, sent even the best of parties into a death spiral.

"You're not . . . you're not a ghost after all . . ."

"Sure I am lady. And now you understand the costume. How else could I have pulled off the whole Ghost of Christmas Future routine?"

"Well . . . Have you ever considered taking a shower?"

"Why should I? I'm a ghost. That's one of the perks of being an apparition. I don't have to bother with bathing."

"Are you sure about that?"

"I wouldn't talk if I were you lady, because you just stepped in dog poop." He pointed to a brown pile on the floor.

"Ugh. Where did that come from? I only saw a cat around here."

To which the ghost host laughed hysterically, seconds before he picked the plastic novelty item up off the floor.

This guy wasn't just a party killer. He was a party annihilator. And if he represented the future of parties everywhere, I had to say, things didn't look so good for the days and years to come.

"All right, let's cut the pranks. Could we please get on with the program? What is it you want to show me? You've already given me a lovely little display of how I'll be all alone in my old age."

Now the ghost raised an eyebrow. "Ha! But there's the rub. Because this is the future according to the path that you're on now. The path where you've given up on hosting parties."

I rolled my eyes. "I know plenty of people who have never even hosted a single Christmas party in their entire lives. What's the big deal? I don't see a bunch of ghost hosts going after them."

"C'mon, lady. They're not as good as you are. They don't have your gifts and talents."

"So what if I never host another party again? Then what?"

"Ah, you know what the Good Book says: 'Do not neglect the gift that is in you.'"

I could hardly believe I was hearing this. "*You're* quoting the Bible, too?"

"Hey, I may be annoying, but I'm not ignorant."

That, in my mind, was debatable.

"So here's a picture of your future, unless you recalculate and take a different route." With those words, the ghost threw something to the ground.

I saw a flash of light just before a thick cloud of smoke filled the air.

I coughed and waved my hands, hoping to clear the smoke enough so that I could see something.

But in a few minutes, the smoke cleared on its own, and I found myself right smack dab in the middle of a fabulous Christmas party. Strands of lights twinkled and sparkled all around the room, and ran between garland and ornaments. Then there was an entire table of nothing but Christmas cookies and candies, with a huge gingerbread house for a centerpiece. Music played in the background, and I could barely make out the song, "God Rest Ye Merry Gentleman." Though it was hard to hear the music at all, considering the loud laughter and conversation that filled the room. Clearly everyone there was having a wonderful time.

I put my hands on my hips and glared at the ghost. "Do you see this? It looks like I *am* hosting a Christmas party. A fantastic Christmas party. In the future. Look around you."

He shook his head. "Oh, I see a great party, all right."

"I don't even have to ask these people to know how much fun they're having."

"It wouldn't do any good, since . . ."

"I know, I know. They can't hear or see me."

"You got it. But there's another reason, there's something else you need to see. Maybe you should sit down first."

Against my better judgment, I sat in the closest chair, just as he'd suggested. And I landed right smack dab on top of a whoopee cushion."

P-p-p-p-b-b-b-l-l-l-u-u-u-u-t-t-t!

The ghost host doubled over in laughter. "Too funny. You gotta love the classics."

My chin nearly hit the floor, especially when the conversation around me ceased and everyone turned in my direction.

"Wait a minute," I said to the ghost. "I thought you said no one could hear or see me."

"They can't. But *everyone* can hear a whoopee cushion. It's a universally recognized sound, in every dimension."

"Give me a break. Did you have something to tell me or not?"

"Of course I do. I just wanted to say that you're not the one hosting this party."

"I'm not?"

"No," the ghost host told me. "Look out the window."

And so I did. That's when I noticed a graveyard outside, with a freshly dug grave. And a brand-new tombstone. One that read, "Carol Frost. Alas, no longer the life of the party."

For a moment or two, I found it hard to breathe.

But at least I was breathing.

"You mean . . . you mean . . ." I sort of sputtered.

"You got it, lady. You're not hosting this party. This is a party that's being hosted at your funeral."

I coughed and choked for a moment. "You mean all these people . . . these total strangers . . . are here to celebrate the fact that I died?"

"Well, sort of. Though I don't think most of them even knew who you were. They're just here for the free food and drinks. But it's a pretty good sendoff, don't you think?"

"No, I don't think it's good at all! It would be nice to know that people felt a little bit of sadness if I was gone. It would be nice to know that someone cared."

"Then, lady, you'd better do something about it. You'd better make some changes in your life. And quick!"

"Take me back, spirit. Take me back now. Right now!"

"Okay, if you insist." And with those words, he threw another smoke bomb to the ground, clouding the air again.

I choked and waved my hands against the smoke.

Above me, I heard a different male voice announce, "Ladies and gentlemen, the fire in the galley has been extinguished and the vent systems will have the smoke removed shortly. Please make sure your seatbelts are fastened as we'll be making an emergency landing."

But *where* were we landing? That was the question.

"Compiling your guest list is every bit as important as deciding on the decorations or the menu for your party. This is a task that can take weeks, and in some cases, months, to prepare. I suggest that you start by creating a large, generic list that can be whittled down as you review the specifics of each potential attendee. Be sure to look at such things as the age, emotional state, and past party performance. Don't be afraid to cross out the names of guests who can be detrimental to your event. Having the right mix of people at your party can make or break your gathering, so never, ever leave such an important task to chance."

(The Complete, Total, Ultimate, Everything-You-Might-Possibly-Want-to-Know Guide to Hosting the Best Christmas Parties Ever by Carol Frost)

CHAPTER 7

I clung tightly to my armrests as the aircraft banked and turned and made a few other interesting maneuvers. I had no idea how the plane had gone from being in pieces to now being completely whole and airborne again. But there were some things that just weren't worth exploring and thinking about, as far as I was concerned.

The smoke quickly started to dissipate as it was sucked out through the air vents. I glanced out the window, at the dark night outside. It had stopped snowing, and for the first

time since the plane had left Cincinnati, I saw stars in the
night sky. One shone especially bright, magnificently so, and I
instantly thought of the star on the night of that very first
Christmas.

The Bethlehem Star.

Christmas had always been a night for miracles, and my
own night had certainly crossed into what could be considered
"miraculous territory." Now I prayed for another miracle,
because more than ever, I wanted to make it home on time.
Not only so I could be there for Christmas, but because . . .
well . . . I had a party to plan. The first Christmas party I'd
thrown since the night Daniel had taken off. So many, many
years ago.

But that was then and this was now. And I was long
overdue when it came to hosting a fantastic Christmas party.

I decided to take the star outside as a sign. A good sign.

The laughing passengers in the rows and rows in front of
me suddenly quieted down and started to sing a very choir-like
version of "Oh, Holy Night." Apparently, their hours of
crooning had practically turned their voices into something
that sounded professional.

And while I enjoyed their music, there was even more
music to my ears when I heard the very announcement that I'd
been dying to hear. "Ladies and Gentlemen, this is your
Captain speaking. We will be landing at Austin-Bergstrom
International Airport in fifteen minutes. Please make sure you
have your seatbacks upright and your tray tables fastened."

And that's when I saw it. The light slowly seeping across
the sky, turning the night into day.

Sunrise.

How long had we been gone?

A flight attendant passed my row, and I waved to get her
attention. "Excuse me, ma'am, could you please tell me what
day this is?"

She smiled and straightened her red Santa hat. "Why, it's the day before Christmas Eve."

"You mean . . . you mean . . . it's the twenty-third?" I could hardly believe my ears. "How can that be? We left on the night of the twentieth."

She shrugged. "Well, we passed the International Dateline a few times. You know, when we were in a holding pattern above the Arctic Circle . . ." She smiled again and passed me a green necklace with red jingle bells dangling from it.

Okay, sure, I knew her explanation made no sense at all, but by now I knew there was no use fighting it. Not after all the things I'd been through in one night. Or rather, what must have been several nights. Instead, I was just glad to be getting home. In one piece. Thankfully, I hadn't missed Christmas completely. But best of all, I still had one more day to organize a Christmas party.

Even so, it was a lot to do in a very short time.

We finally landed, and much to my amazement, I seemed to be the only one at the baggage carousel, picking up my suitcase. All the other Christmas revelers had disappeared. I wondered if they had connecting flights.

Or if they'd even been real at all.

I got a few strange glances as I swished through the airport, dragging my luggage in my long, red gown and my updo that had partially fallen down. But it really didn't matter that much to me. After all, I'd seen much stranger things myself in one night than I had in a whole lifetime.

Besides that, I was on a mission of sorts.

I called my daughter from the car as I headed north out of Austin, to my home in Georgetown. "I really need you to be home tomorrow night. For Christmas," I told her.

"Um . . . no . . . I don't think I'll be there," my daughter hemmed and hawed. "Dylan just isn't comfortable with the whole Christmas thing, Mom."

"I don't give a rodent's patootie whether Dylan likes it or not. You've only dated him a few weeks and he's not part of this family . . . yet. But you are. And I need you to come home to help me throw a Christmas party. A huge Christmas party. Bring Dylan or don't bring Dylan. It doesn't matter to me."

"Mom, you're throwing a party? A Christmas party? You haven't thrown one of those since I was little."

"I know," I said with a sigh. "It's been way too long . . . Now, are you in?"

Clara laughed. "I'll be there in the morning."

"Great. Thanks, honey."

My next call was to my son.

Joey answered in his sleepiest voice. "Yeah, Mom, what is it?"

"I'll be home pretty soon, and I want you to get out the vacuum and get to work. Start cleaning the house."

"Seriously, Mom, have you lost it? I'm not your maid."

"No, but you're living under my roof, and at my expense. At the very least, you can earn your keep around there. And you can start by cleaning the house."

"But I was up half the night."

"Playing video games?"

"And texting my friends."

"Well, you're a grown man, and that's no way for a grown man to live."

"Mom, I'm a kid."

"Honey, I hate to tell you this, but your childhood ended a long time ago. My father already had a thriving business by the time he was your age. He was married and had a child to support."

"Yeah, but things were easier back then."

I chuckled. "Oh no they weren't. Now it's time for you to embrace adulthood. We'll talk about some ground rules when I get home. But for now, I want you to start cleaning."

"Mom, what is wrong with you? You're acting entirely weird."

That made me smile. My son didn't even begin to know the meaning of the word "weird." Weird was having a conversation with your dead friend and spending a night with three ghost hosts and losing a couple of days in the process. And that was just for starters.

I answered Joey with a chuckle. "I'm just doing a few things that I should have done long ago. Starting with hosting a party tomorrow night. And I need your help."

"A Christmas party? You haven't had one of those since I was a kid. I mean, when I was *really* a kid."

"I know, son."

"Mom, why'd you ever quit hosting your parties? You were really good at it. Everyone loved them. I remember how much fun they were."

I sighed. "I know. They were fun. And looking back now, I wish I'd done some things differently. But after your father left, I let the pain of the divorce affect me for far too long."

"Yeah, Mom, that *was* when you sort of checked out of things."

Funny, but I didn't realize my son had noticed. That he'd been so aware.

"I'm sorry, Joseph. I guess we all have bad things happen to us in life. But we can't let those moments define us and ruin the rest of our lives. We can't let them determine who we are."

"Whoa . . . Mom, you're getting a little deep here. But don't sweat it. We all got waylaid by what Dad did."

"Thanks for saying that, Joey. You're a good kid."

"Does that mean I can go back to sleep?"

"Nope. I need your help."

"All right then. I'll start cleaning."

A smile crossed my lips.

I was about to hang up when Joey added, "Oh, Mom?"

"Yes, son?"

"Welcome back."

Minutes later I pulled into the parking lot of my local grocery store. I didn't even need a list, since, even now, I knew the items I needed by heart. Probably because I'd hosted a million Christmas parties in the past, and my standard grocery list was practically burned into my brain.

And if I thought I'd gotten strange looks at the airport, it was nothing compared to the looks I got now. But I didn't let that deter me. Instead, I raced through the aisles, grabbing a couple of hams and a dozen Cornish game hens. And plenty of ingredients for baking. By nightfall, I planned to have batches and batches of my special sugar cookies ready to go.

With a grocery cart loaded to the brim and practically spilling over, I pulled into a checkout line.

The tattooed young woman behind the cash register stared at me with wide eyes. "Wow, lady, that's a lot of stuff. Are you having a party?"

"Yes, I am," I told her firmly. "I'm hosting a Christmas party tomorrow night."

"Geez, lady, you must have a whole lotta people coming over. You sure waited till the last minute to get all this stuff. You're cutting it pretty close, aren't you?"

"Maybe. But I just decided to throw my party this morning."

Her eyeliner-darkened eyes went wide. "Seriously? How did you get all those people to come over on Christmas Eve? People usually have plans by then."

Much as I hated to admit it, this young woman had a point. How would I ever be able to round up a large group of party guests at this late hour?

"Well . . ." I said, swallowing hard. "I haven't *actually* invited anyone yet."

Her pierced lip dropped open and her eyes practically bugged out. "Are you kidding me, lady? You'll never get anyone to come to your party now. You sure you want to buy all this food?"

I glanced at the huge mound of groceries that I'd amassed after running up and down the aisles. Unfortunately, it seemed I'd also run smack dab into a very solid wall. One called reality.

But after spending who knew how many days in a very unreal world, I could see how reality might be way overrated. And I wasn't about to give up on my very recent plan to return to my Christmas party hosting roots.

Not now.

Not after I'd finally made the decision to host a party again. Not after years and years of being dormant in the at-home entertaining department.

But if I couldn't pull off a party now, that meant it would be an entire year before I had the chance to host another one. And I had no intention of waiting that long. After all, I'd waited long enough.

By now there were several people in line behind me. I glanced at the next person, a rather handsome man who looked dashing in his uniform. He was solidly built, silver-haired, and about my age. His nameplate read, "Colonel Christopher Cringl."

Minus the "Colonel" part, it was probably a name that didn't bode well on the playground when he was a child.

He smiled, and I was just sure I saw momentary flashes of light bounce off his perfect white teeth, much like any Prince Charming in any fairytale movie.

"I know who you can invite to a last minute Christmas party," he informed me in a raspy baritone. "Every military base in the country has people who would be grateful to spend Christmas Eve in a civilian's home, including soldiers from Ft. Hood. I could have dozens of people rounded up and transported to your location in a hurry."

"You could?" I murmured as I stood mesmerized by his vivid blue eyes. I quickly reminded myself to blink and stop staring.

He nodded. "Yes, ma'am. In fact, I wouldn't mind being in attendance myself. If you'd be agreeable."

"That would be wonderful," I managed to mutter.

Then the woman standing in line behind him raised her hand. "I can help, too." She touched red-painted nails to teased and lacquered blonde hair. "I compose creative obituaries for the newspaper. I know a wealth of widows and widowers without family who would love to attend an at-home party. In fact, they would probably find it to be a shelter in a storm. A junket on their journey through despair. A sweet refuge from the sorrows they've been suffering."

"That would be lovely," I nodded, amazed at the way things were going.

Now the man behind her leaned around and raised his hand, too. "I run a group for the recently divorced. Christmas can be pretty rough after a marriage breaks up, especially that first Christmas. I'm guessing a lot of my group members would jump at the idea of having somewhere wonderful to go for Christmas."

Didn't I know it. After all, I'd been the poster child for the devastation that comes from a divorce, and I'd let my suffering go on for far longer than I should have. So now, what could be nicer than helping another divorcee find their feet again? And for that matter, what could be better than helping the newly bereaved adjust to the world without a loved one? Not to mention, how could I pass up the chance to show respect and appreciation for members of our military?

Though to be honest, I wasn't sure who was helping whom. After all, I was getting the help I needed by helping someone else. Funny how that worked.

And it was also pretty interesting how the three people behind me just happened to show up in the right place at the right time. What were the odds of that? Probably pretty slim. Yet deep down in my heart I knew this was no coincidence. Not after all the bizarre things I'd been through the night before.

I smiled at my three new chums before turning back to the checkout girl. "To answer your question, yes, absolutely. I do need all these groceries. I only hope I have enough for the party I'm about to give." Then I flashed her my sweetest smile.

Whereby she shrugged and started to scan my pile of food.

After everything had been bagged and put in my cart, I waited until the others were finished checking out, before we all exchanged pertinent information and made the necessary arrangements. Kyle, the divorce group guy, and Kari, the obit author, and Chris . . . well, no need to describe Chris any further . . . all said they'd start contacting people right away and email me with their guest lists.

Then we said our goodbyes, and I wheeled my loaded grocery cart to the car, enjoying that old familiar sensation that I always got before hosting a party. It was a special, private moment of exhilaration, one that came from knowing the joy a good Christmas party could bring to my guests. And this time I would be bringing that joy to people who might otherwise spend this special holiday alone.

But exhilaration quickly turned to anxiety, and my heart began to pound like it was going to bounce right out of my chest. Because it had been a long time since I'd even hosted any kind of party at all, let alone a truly fantastic Christmas party. Now the question was, could I dust off my old hosting skills and pull off a truly memorable event? Especially when time wasn't exactly on my side?

It was a good thing that Christmas was the season of miracles. Because one thing was for sure — I was definitely going to need a few in the upcoming hours.

"Setting up for your party can be every bit as enjoyable as the party itself, so be sure to allow yourself plenty of time to complete your preparations in a relaxed and upbeat fashion. Never let yourself become stressed out or uptight. And make sure you schedule a little extra time for any unforeseen mishaps. After all, you want to be your most ebullient and entertaining self when that first guest rings your doorbell."

(The Complete, Total, Ultimate, Everything-You-Might-Possibly-Want-to-Know Guide to Hosting the Best Christmas Parties Ever by Carol Frost)

CHAPTER 8

At long last, I pulled into my garage, and immediately started dragging both groceries and luggage into the kitchen. I was so overjoyed to be home that I nearly fell on my knees and kissed the ground.

Which in my case would have been my hardwood floor.

And were it not for a small layer of dust on that very floor, I might have actually gone through with the whole ground-kissing ritual. Because I couldn't remember the last time I'd been so happy to set foot inside my ornately-decorated house. Especially since there'd been so many moments the night (or nights) before when I wasn't even sure if I'd make it back in one piece.

But I didn't have time to wax sentimental. Or wax anything, for that matter. Instead, I went right back to hauling in enough groceries to feed a small army, something that may not have been too far off the mark, depending on how many people my new Army friend invited.

I started stashing the perishables in my oversized refrigerator, just as my two fluffy Norwegian Forest cats trotted in. Dancer was a lovely calico and Blitzen was a Mackerel tabby, and both were rescues from a local group. And both were blinking the sleep from their eyes. I guessed they'd been napping somewhere.

The kitties purred and wove around my long red dress as I put the last of the food in cold storage. Then I leaned over to pet them, getting chirrups and meows in return. At least someone was glad I was home.

Now I began to wonder where my son was hiding out. Hopefully, he wasn't lost in another video game, instead of cleaning house like I'd asked him to.

"Joey!" I called. "I'm home! Where are you?"

And that's when I heard it. A loud groan coming from the family room. I raced into the room with my long skirts swishing as I went. Dancer and Blitzen hurried along behind me.

There I found Joey, lying on the couch, with his right leg elevated and his ankle the size of a cantaloupe.

"Hi, Mom. Glad you're home."

"What happened . . .?" I started to ask, right before I glanced around the room and pieced together the obvious clues.

Starting with the Christmas tree and stepladder. Both lying on their sides.

What a guy wouldn't do to get out of housecleaning.

"I wanted to surprise you with a Christmas tree," Joey murmured as he cringed.

"That was very thoughtful of you, son. But it'll have to wait. Right now it looks like we're headed to the ER. Let's get you to the car."

"Geez, Mom. Really? I'm sure it's just a sprain. No need to go all *Grey's Anatomy* on me."

I shook my head. "With the way that thing's swollen, I'm betting it's broken. Can you stand on it at all?"

"No. But that doesn't mean anything."

"There's only one way to know for sure. We've got to get it checked out."

An hour later, there I was, waiting in an ER examining room while Joey was being wheeled away for an x-ray. Funny how he'd gone from suffering in silence to moaning in all out agony the minute a pretty young nurse had walked in. In fact, his pain had mysteriously increased with every sympathetic sound she'd cooed. He, of course, made sure she was well aware of his stoic fight through his suffering.

I fought the urge to roll my eyes when he'd whispered to the nurse, "I only hope I'll be able to walk again some day."

Whereby she responded with, "Oh, you poor thing."

Then he jutted out his chin and pretended to blink back tears. "I was just trying to help out my mom when the accident happened."

"You're such a good guy, helping your mom," she said gently. "I hope she appreciates you. But don't you worry, we'll get you fixed up right away."

He didn't so much as wave goodbye to me as she whisked him off to Radiology.

Needless to say, as I sat there waiting, I was pretty sure my red dress probably looked as bad as Joey's ankle. And if I'd thought I'd gotten strange looks at the airport, it was nothing compared to what I'd gotten when we walked into the hospital. Especially since half my hair had fallen down completely, and I was long overdue for a shower and a change of clothes.

Worst of all, for the first time in my entire party-planning life, I was starting to wonder how I would pull off my big bash the next night. Just dusting off my long-dormant party skills alone had put me under plenty of pressure. But watching the clock count down as though it were in a race against time itself had sent my stress level into the stratosphere.

Some great party guru I was turning out to be.

The text that suddenly pinged on my phone didn't help, either. Though in all honesty, I did feel a little tingling sensation when I noticed it was from my new Army officer friend, Chris Cringl.

"Got thirty people coming over," he wrote. "We're all looking forward to it."

"Terrific!" I texted back. "Please email the list to me, and I'll get nametags made up after I get home."

"You're not home yet?" came his immediate reply. "Having car trouble?"

"Nope," I texted back. "I'm at the hospital. With my son. He hurt his leg. Probably broken. It's being x-rayed now."

"Sorry to hear that. Do you need to cancel the party?" he asked.

"The party is still on. It's too late to turn back now," I typed with all the bravado I could muster. "Gotta go. The doctor is coming in now. See you and your bunch tomorrow!"

I turned my phone off and dropped it into my purse, just as Dr. Greench slipped into the room. He had the thickest hair I'd ever seen on another human being, and it covered his arms, hands, head, and chin.

"It's not good," he informed me with a scowl. "Joseph has fractured his fibula. He'll be on crutches over Christmas."

"Well . . ." I sighed. "It's not his first broken bone. So I guess we know the drill."

The doctor raised a hairy eyebrow. "How did this accident occur?"

I scrunched up my nose. "He was trying to put up a Christmas tree."

That's when the doctor turned a little green, like he'd suddenly become sick to his stomach. "Oh, Christmas! The holiday I hate the most. We see more broken bones in here thanks to mishaps while decorating for the holidays. Then there's food poisoning from ingesting raw cookie dough. Not to mention, injuries from electronic toys gone awry. It's just one endless stream of patients, all season long. It's a horrible, dangerous time of year. I would be happy if Christmas never came again!"

My eyes practically popped out of my head. "So I suspect you're not a fan of Christmas parties, either."

To which he raised his hands in the air. "Horrors of all horrors. Why anyone would even consider celebrating such misery is beyond me."

Thankfully, he'd expressed his viewpoint before I'd invited him to my big event the next night.

And while his attitude certainly appalled me, oddly enough, it also made me dig in my heels with more determination than ever to host my party. Especially after I got texts from Kyle and Kari while I waited for the medical staff to finish up with Joey. Both Kyle and Kari told me they'd be bringing between fifteen to twenty guests. Meaning, it was too late for me to back out now, even if I wanted to. So, one way or another, I would be hosting a Christmas party the following night.

Now the question was, what kind of party would I be hosting? One worthy of my book that was published so long ago? Or one that would go down in history as the worst get-together known to humankind?

Four hours after we'd left for the hospital, I helped a smiling, chuckling Joey into the house. It was amazing what a broken ankle could do for a guy. He didn't seem the least bit upset that he was on crutches and now sporting a red and white candy-cane striped cast. One his new nurse friend, Emily, had gone to great pains to decorate. No, mostly he was just elated that he'd gotten Emily's phone number.

That, and I'm sure the pain pills he'd been given probably helped his attitude a little, too.

I got him settled on the couch, whereby he promptly fell asleep.

Then, at long last, I went to my room, took off my red dress, and treated myself to a quick shower. I fought the urge to also take a quick nap, but unfortunately, sleep was a luxury I just couldn't afford at the moment. Instead, I opted for a strong cup of coffee while I started to mix cookie dough. Lots and lots of cookie dough. Before long, I had a huge bowl of it chilling in the refrigerator.

With that task checked off my list, I went into the family room to tackle the Christmas tree. I managed to get it upright in its stand with a little maneuvering, and, with a minimum of scratches to my arms. Amazingly, Joey slept through the whole thing. But at least he'd picked a very nice, full nine-foot tree for us.

Apparently, the kitties must have thought so too, because I had barely started to tighten the bolts in the stand to hold the tree in place when Dancer burst into the room, followed by her brother, Blitzen. With a wild gleam in her eyes, Dancer practically flew for the base of that tree. She latched on and went straight up the trunk, with the momentum of a Saturn V rocket.

Just as she reached the top, the entire tree started to sway. Dancer dug in her claws and held on for dear life, doing her best to compensate each time the tree swung back and forth. I immediately jumped onto the ladder and tried to reach through the branches to grab the trunk, hoping to steady the tree myself.

But it was no use. Seconds later, the whole thing went tumbling over.

It landed on the floor with a definite *whump*! Dancer went zooming off while Blitzen tried to weave his way through the branches.

Joey woke up, mumbled a few words and then fell back to sleep once more.

Right before the phone rang.

It was my boss, Mr. Pfunn. "Carol, dear girl, my wife and I are stranded in Dallas. At the airport. We were flying to Phoenix to spend Christmas with our son's family, but they're having a rotten storm and we can't get in. And the airlines are booked solid for the next few days, so we can't even get home. Plus there isn't a hotel room available in this entire city. How far do you live from Dallas? Would you mind a few extras for Christmas? I'd sure hate for my wife to have to spend Christmas in an airport."

"Uh . . . uh . . . uh . . ." I sputtered for a moment or two.

After all, handling a couple of houseguests just seemed like a complete impossibility at the moment. I barely had time to get ready for my party . . . no, scratch that . . . I didn't even have time to get ready for my party, let alone get things set up in my guestroom. Last I could recall, my guestroom had become a repository for the mountains of Pfunn Party Supplies samples that I'd collected over the years. I couldn't honestly remember what the décor of that room even looked like by now. It would take me hours to get it cleaned up and put together for a couple of guests.

But this was my boss, and he had truly taken me in, so to speak, when I was desperate. How could I turn him and his wife away, especially since they had nowhere else to go at Christmas? Hadn't we all learned from that whole "no room at the inn" thing so many years ago?

So while my heart started to pound in panic on the inside, outwardly I forced Christmas cheer into my voice. "Why, of course, Mr. Pfunn. I'd be happy to have you and Mrs. Pfunn come stay with us. By the way, I'm hosting a Christmas party tomorrow night . . ."

"Splendid! Looking forward to it! We'll be there in less than four hours, provided we don't hit heavy traffic," he practically bellowed into the phone, before hanging up.

I guess that meant he had my address and directions to my house. As well as a rental car.

With visions of a *fantastic* Christmas party quickly fading from my mind, I raced up the staircase and into my guestroom. I turned on the light and started piling boxes and samples into haphazard stacks. Then I ran with those stacks and stashed them into my walk-in attic, keeping out the Christmas decorations, of course.

A few hours later, the room was de-cluttered, the sheets were changed and the bathroom sparkled. In other words, the place looked pretty spiffy, if not rather nice. In fact, I'd forgotten what an inviting room it was, and I knew Mr. and Mrs. Pfunn would be perfectly comfortable staying there. I pulled the top two drawers of the bureau open, to make sure there was a place for them to store their things.

And that's when I saw it.

The letter.

One that Daniel had written to me right after he ran off with my so-called friend. A "Dear John" letter. Or in my case, a "Dear Carol" letter. The second I saw it, I instantly felt like I'd been dunked into ice-cold water. I didn't remember even keeping the letter, let alone stashing it in my guest room.

Of all the times for it to resurface, why did it have to show up now?

I pulled the letter from the envelope and started to read, each word like a knife stabbing at my heart. So why did the mere sight of his handwritten words immediately take me back to that time and place? Especially since the Ghost Host of Christmas Past had already forced me to face my feelings about that night. She'd thrust me right into the scene and made me live through the horror and heartache all over again, supposedly so I could put it behind me for good.

So why did the pain of my very last Christmas party feel so raw right now? And for that matter, why had I been such a fool to even think about hosting a party tomorrow night? Or any other night. My Christmas Party hosting days had ended in disaster and were obviously something I should have left behind me.

And now I had to wonder why those ghost hosts had even shown up in my life at all. Had their presence been nothing but a cruel joke? And why, oh why, had I let them convince me to host a Christmas party again, something that would only set me up for failure?

Tears pricked at my eyes, and more than anything, I wanted to cancel my party and forget the whole day had ever happened.

And then the doorbell rang.

The Pfunns must have arrived in world record time. How could they possibly be here already?

"To make your guests feel at home, treat them like they're part of the family, by giving each one a role and responsibility. For instance, you might assign one to be on 'Cookie Detail,' and ask them to make sure the plates of iced sugar cookies are well stocked. Other guests can be in charge of serving eggnog and making mixed drinks. Nothing adds to the merriment like getting everyone to play a part, so never be afraid to delegate. A good hostess dispenses duties as easily as she dons her diamonds before the doorbell first rings."

(The Complete, Total, Ultimate, Everything-You-Might-Possibly-Want-to-Know Guide to Hosting the Best Christmas Parties Ever by Carol Frost)

CHAPTER 9

It took fourteen major muscle groups for me to affix a smile on my face as I opened my wide front door. "Good evening, Mr. and Mrs. Pfunn," I managed to coo. "Welcome to my home . . ."

But I'd barely uttered the words when I realized it wasn't the Pfunns who had rung my doorbell. Instead, I found a group of a dozen men and women, all complete strangers, standing on my front porch.

Before I could so much as mutter a, "May I help you?" the curly-haired lady in front held out her hand to shake.

I put my hand in hers and she pumped it up and down several times, like she was churning butter. "*Ooooooh*! My goodness! Carol, I can't believe I'm meeting you in the flesh. What a complete honor this is!"

"Why, thank you," I said in return, still fighting to keep my smile in place. "And your name is?"

"I'm Daphne," she gushed. "Your number one fan. And we're with Kyle's divorce group."

Now the light began to dawn, which also sent my blood pressure soaring. Especially when I realized that Kyle must have relayed my message wrong. Clearly he'd told his group the party was to take place tonight. That meant this jovial bunch before me had arrived a whole twenty-four hours early.

As a general rule, no hostess enjoys any guest who even arrives a half-hour to an hour ahead of time, but arriving twenty-four hours early had crossed into uncharted territory. Not that I should have been surprised, considering, in the history of "things that could go wrong," this day had chalked up a pretty sizable list. If ever there was a time in my life when I could have happily crawled under a rock, this was it.

But with no gigantic boulder nearby and the revelers on my doorstep anticipating a party, I had no choice but to stand up tall and just deal with the situation.

"I'm terribly sorry," I told them. "But I'm afraid there's been a mix-up. The party doesn't start until . . ."

The man behind her waved me off. "We know, we know. The party is tomorrow night."

The red-haired lady beside him spoke up. "But Kyle got a text from some guy in the Army. Chris, I think it was. He told Kyle that your son had been injured. And he says it happened right when you were putting your party together."

Another man was already nodding. "Then Kyle texted all of us and told us what happened."

"That's right," Daphne said, with a smile that seemed to be growing by the second. "And since I have your book completely memorized . . ."

Now the group behind her raised their hands. "We've all read your book."

"Used it for years and years and years," another woman added.

"Know it by heart," yet another lady chimed in.

"So we decided to come to your rescue," the man behind her said. "Since you basically taught us what to do, through the pages of your book."

"That's right," Daphne finished. "We're here to help."

"You've all read my book . . .?" I sort of gasped. "It came out so long ago . . ."

The whole group responded by talking at once, with plenty of choruses of "love that book," and "my favorite," and "I couldn't live without it."

I, on the other hand, suddenly lost my ability to even form words at all.

Then without being invited in, Daphne sort of scootched her way around me and into my foyer, her eyes tracing every inch of the space. "This area will definitely need lights. Tons and tons of lights. As Chapter Three of your book states, and I quote, 'Nothing helps create the proper ambience like varying degrees, styles, and colors of lighting. Strands of mini-twinkle lights are the best, and be sure to stay away from over-bright LEDs.'"

Murmurs of "yes, yes," arose from the rest of the group. And that seemed to be the cue for them to just saunter on in. I pulled the door open wider and took a step back, to avoid being stampeded by these people who were clearly on a mission.

Now Daphne motioned toward my staircase banister and the upstairs balcony that protruded out and above the first floor. This simple action was enough to initiate a rather enthusiastic discussion from the group about garland, poinsettia wreaths, and the right color of twinkle lights to entwine through the staircase spindles.

Daphne turned to one of the men. "Larry, have you got the lights and garland?"

He held up a huge box. "Brought it all. Just like it says in Chapter Four. And I included plenty of extension cords, like Chapter Seven suggested."

"Where is your vacuum?" another lady asked me. "Chapter Two of your book says, 'Nothing makes a guest feel more welcome than a spotlessly clean home.'"

I pointed to a closet at the end of the hall.

"I'll take mop duty," another man chimed in. "I was in the Navy and I've swabbed a deck or two in my day. And Chapter Two talks about the importance of squeaky-clean floors. In fact, it said a guest's fun should never be interrupted by stepping on something sticky."

A woman dressed in workout gear displayed a tool belt with organic window cleaner and furniture spray as well as dust rags and a squeegee. "And Chapter Two also says, 'Never, ever use harsh cleaning chemicals the day before your party. You want your home to smell like sugar cookies and vanilla candles. Not like a chemical plant has just opened up next door.'"

By this time, I was completely flabbergasted. "You are all so kind to help with my party, but I'm afraid I don't even know your names . . ."

That's when an older woman showed me a box filled with colored paper, glue, sequins, rhinestones, scissors and more. "Not to worry. I've got that covered. Chapter Five talks about the importance of having artistic nametags for all. So not only will guests enjoy wearing them, but others will enjoy looking at them, too. And no one will get stressed out trying to remember the other people's names."

"Don't forget," the man beside her added, "you're supposed to include one interesting tidbit about each person on their nametag. For an easy conversation starter."

A woman with a huge ponytail nodded. "I always considered that idea to be one of the most clever things about the whole book."

The petite woman next to her shook her head. "No, I think the most clever thing in the whole book was in Chapter Ten."

A sandy-haired man raised his pale eyebrows. "Yup. I know just what you're talking about. Under the heading, 'Playing with your food.'"

"That's it!" The petite woman's eyes went wide and she held up a grocery bag. "It was under the subheading, 'Fun with Phyllo,' where she used strawberries and Phyllo Dough to create miniature Poinsettias. I brought everything I need to make up a whole batch. I bake that recipe every year at Christmas."

She turned to me with a huge smile. "If you don't mind, I'll just head to the kitchen to get to work. Would you please point me in the right direction?"

And on it went. Before I knew it, someone was running my vacuum cleaner and other people had started to weave garland and ribbon and lights around my banister and through the staircase spindles. Others had started to dust while still more people pulled decorations from the bags and boxes they'd carried in. And I'd yet to even step away from my still-open front door.

Out of the corner of my eye, I now spotted an older woman waving to me as she raced up the sidewalk. "Oh my goodness! It's you! It's really you! Carol Frost in the flesh. I never thought I'd see the day where I got to meet you in person. You're my favorite author. I don't know what I would have done without your book. My late husband loved Christmas, and I put on the best parties thanks to you. It's so lovely to meet you in person. I'm Gertrude."

I took her hand in mine. "It's wonderful to meet you, too, Gertrude," I said, all the while wondering how she happened to be on my doorstep.

"Kari called me," she quickly explained, as though she'd read my mind. "Twice. The first time to tell me about the party tomorrow night. And the second time to tell me about your son being in the hospital. Evidently, she heard it from some military man, who said you could really use some help right now. So I rushed right over. I've been making your famous Christmas cookies every year since your book came out. My friends and family absolutely rave about them, and I thought I'd help out by making some over here for your party. I'm guessing you already have the ingredients."

I laughed. "Even better. I've got the cookie dough chilling in the refrigerator."

She nodded. "Yes, of course you do. I would expect no less. But if you don't mind, I brought my favorite cookie cutters. After all, Chapter Ten in your book talks about putting your own special signature to each cookie."

"Sounds wonderful. I'm looking forward to it."

"I'll just get to work in the kitchen."

It was a good thing I had double ovens, since my kitchen was about to get crowded.

Not to mention, the rest of my house was, too. Because, as I stood there near my front door, little by little, more and more people trickled in to help with the party preparations. Before long, I had a small army of helpers, each happily contributing in their own way.

And speaking of an army, or rather, "the Army," the man who had orchestrated this entire set-up "operation" now sauntered up the walk, followed by five huge young men. Judging from their haircuts and posture, I was pretty sure the other men were soldiers, too, though they were dressed in their "civvies." Each one must have been at least six-and-a-half-feet tall. Chris, who wasn't quite that height, led the charge with a

Christmas bouquet of red roses and white lilies in a red crystal vase.

A flower arrangement that looked very familiar.

I smiled at him when he came closer. "Well, if it isn't my hero. I'm told I have you to thank for sending all this help my way."

He grinned as he stepped onto my porch. "I might have had something to do with it." He handed the flowers to me. "These are for you. Permission to enter the premises, ma'am? I've brought even more helpers."

"Permission granted," I laughed. "How could I possibly say no to a handsome man bearing such a beautiful bouquet?"

"That was my strategy." He smiled even broader, and I was just sure I saw flashes of light coming from his teeth. "Half the people I rounded up for this party recognized your name. I didn't know you were a famous author when I met you at the grocery store."

"It's been a long time since I've written that book."

"The library still has a copy. I checked it out, and there were a few pages on the perfect bouquets for Christmas. When I showed it to the florist, she knew it by heart. She said it was the gold standard for all Christmas bouquets."

"That is very sweet of you to say. *And* to bring me these flowers."

His eyes held mine for a moment, before he added, "Have you ever thought about writing a second book?"

I laughed. "Well . . . let's just say the idea has been on my mind lately."

"Glad to hear it. By the way, I rounded up this bunch of big guys to decorate your tree for you."

Now I understood why he'd shown up with such an "elevated" bunch. Not a one of them would have the least bit of trouble reaching the upper branches, let alone, putting the star on top of the tree. There would be no ladders needed, which also meant there was no chance for injuries.

I gave them directions to the family room, all the while wondering if a bunch of big Army guys decorating a Christmas tree would be enough to wake my son.

They had barely disappeared around the corner when I turned to see a Christmas tree moving up my front walkway. As it approached, I noticed it was concealing the middle-aged man who carried it.

He set the artificial tree down on my front porch and introduced himself. "I'm Ralph," he told me. "I got an email from Kari. It's very kind of you to host this party. My late wife was a big fan of yours. I can't use this Christmas tree anymore, since I've downsized. And I knew she'd want you to have it. I've brought the decorations and everything. They're in my van."

"Wonderful," I told him, just as I spotted Daphne waving from my staircase.

"We could use that tree up here on the balcony," she hollered down to us. "According to Chapter Three, all lights should ultimately lead to a Christmas tree of one kind or another."

Minutes later, another widower brought in an antique aluminum tree, complete with a lighted color wheel. I suggested he set it up in the living room.

Meanwhile, the scent of cookies baking filled my house, and I could hear the whir of kitchen appliances coming from my gourmet kitchen. Light strands were being plugged in everywhere, with regular room lights being turned off momentarily to test the glow. Mr. and Mrs. Pfunn arrived, and someone magically materialized to carry their luggage up to my guest room. Minutes later, the Pfunns came back downstairs, carrying loads of Pfunn Party Supply decorations. They immediately joined in with the rest of the crowd to help deck the halls, so to speak. Mr. Pfunn laughed in his usual "ho-ho-ho" style.

Not long after that, he made a point of pulling me aside. "I'm so glad you decided to host a party after all, Carol."

"Me, too, Mr. Pfunn."

He spread his arms wide in a motion that tugged at the strands of twinkle lights wrapped around his arms, as he gestured at all the busyness around us. "In case you haven't noticed, all these people here have taken a page from your book."

That made me smile. "It looks that way, doesn't it?"

"Yes, it does," he said, with his jolly St. Nick cheeks glowing pink. "That's why I'd like you to write a second book, Carol, my dear. I'd like to publish it under the Pfunn Party Supplies label. Then I'll add it to our inventory."

I gasped. I could hardly believe my ears. "Why, that would be wonderful, Mr. Pfunn. In fact, I even started thinking about writing a second book . . . just recently. And I certainly have plenty of notes and ideas left over, things I didn't have room for in my first book."

"Outstanding! I can hardly wait. We'll sell trillions of copies. People will be so happy to get your second book. Just look around you. Look how much joy you've brought to people. And with a second book, you'll be spreading even more of the Christmas Spirit."

I had to say, he had a point. Because people were laughing and talking and clearly having a fantastic time. It appeared the pre-party alone had turned into quite the party itself.

"Okay, Mr. Pfunn," I said. "I'll get to work on my next book right after Christmas."

"Wonderful. That's the best Christmas present anyone could give me." He let out another "ho-ho-ho" laugh and went off to help his wife decorate the fireplace mantel in the living room.

I smiled and strolled to my family room. There I found my son staring bleary-eyed at an almost completely decorated tree, while three of Chris's soldiers hung the last of the ornaments. The tallest of the young men reached up to put the star on the very top.

I was amazed that anyone could do such a thing.

It appeared that Dancer and Blitzen were too, as they both sat at attention on a nearby console table, fascinated, and obviously on their best behavior. I guessed they weren't about to attempt another tree takedown with these soldiers around. In fact, I was pretty sure I heard both kitties purring in admiration, as I noticed them receiving the occasional chin scratch or ear rub from the young men.

"Thank you for all your help," I said to these young soldiers. "I'm afraid I didn't get your names when you walked in."

I heard, "Tom and Matt," from two of them. But the one who had put the star in place simply stood there and grinned.

"His name is Tim," said Tom.

Matt laughed. "But we all call him 'Tiny.'"

"Tiny Tim?" I repeated.

Seriously?

Images of my three ghost hosts flashed through my mind.

"Yes, ma'am," Tim said with a smile. "And I would like to thank you for inviting us to your home. It's so nice for servicemen and women to have a place to go on Christmas. If you don't mind, I was wondering if I might say a blessing tomorrow night when the party starts. Since I'm studying to become an Army chaplain."

"That would be lovely," I told him.

"Thank you, ma'am," he said, continuing to smile.

I looked at the young faces before me. "Does anyone know where Chris might be?"

"Yes, ma'am," Matt answered. "He went to your dining room."

I was about to leave when Joey waved his hand to get my attention. "Mom, I think these pain pills are too strong. They're making me hallucinate. Because it looks like three soldiers are decorating our Christmas tree."

"It's okay, son," I said as I patted his arm. "Three soldiers aren't decorating our tree. Because actually, they're all finished now."

Joey blinked a few times and shook his head. "Huh? What? Wait a minute . . ."

I left my befuddled son and headed for my dining room. There I saw someone had laid out an elegant gold brocade tablecloth, and chargers and plates were being positioned exactly as I'd written about in Chapter Ten of my book. But I also saw two of Chris's soldiers on ladders, while Chris was near the entry.

"Close your eyes," he told me. "I've got a surprise for you."

I laughed and did exactly that. I heard scuffling from ladders and a few other sounds before I felt his warmth beside me, and his hand slid across my shoulders. My insides turned more molten than my famous peppermint, dark-chocolate lava cake.

"Okay," he murmured into my ear. "You can open your eyes now."

So I did.

And I immediately gasped.

For there, across the high ceiling of my dining room, were strands and strands of white twinkle lights, all connecting to the top of my chandelier chain and then pulled out in swags to the corners and edges of the room, before hanging down the walls. The effect was dramatic, fairy-tale like, as the light cast a magical warm glow across the room.

"Do you like it?" he asked as he gave my shoulders a squeeze.

"I love it," I sighed. "It's stunning. Such a wonderful idea."

And one that most definitely did not come from my book.

"In the end, after the food has been set out so carefully, and the lights and decorations placed so lovingly around the house, take a moment to listen to the laughter and the conversations all around you. Let it remind you of the reason you hosted this party in the first place. Then give yourself a pat on the back, because people who host parties are risk takers, adventurers, and willing to selflessly do something special for their fellow human beings. So whether a party goes according to plan or not, know that you did your part in spreading the joy of the season, and passing along the Christmas Spirit to all."

(The Complete, Total, Ultimate, Everything-You-Might-Possibly-Want-to-Know Guide to Hosting the Best Christmas Parties Ever by Carol Frost)

CHAPTER 10

The next night, bright stars twinkled in a dark navy sky as the first of my guests arrived for the party. I greeted them at the door, wearing a holiday gown of silver and gold lamé, with crystal beads for added shimmer. And while I got plenty of compliments on my attire, I heard even more *oooohs* and *aaaahs* as everyone stepped into my house and saw the finished product, so to speak, of the hard work of a whole herd of helpers. Because my house had been completely transformed into a Christmas wonderland, with twinkle lights and tinsel sparkling everywhere. Perfectly decorated Christmas trees stood majestically, with lights blinking in time to the music of Nat King Cole, whose velvet voice crooned through speakers hidden strategically around the house.

After greeting each guest, I turned them over to Grace, one of the widows whom Kari had invited. Grace quickly safety-pinned homemade poinsettia, snowflake, or Christmas tree nametags on each person. Then the guests were passed on to Daphne, who handed out "party maps," showing a layout of all the rooms where guests could wander, including the location of the bathrooms.

The map, a la Chapter Fourteen of my book, also listed points of interest in my home that each guest might enjoy. Things such as my antique French crystal Nativity set on the fireplace mantel, and my Vincent Van Gogh-like painting in the hallway, one that beautifully depicted the three Wise Men traveling by the light of the Bethlehem Star. Also included on the map were the locations of all three of my Christmas trees, as well as the history behind each one. And for those feeling the need to convene with Santa, they could find him in the family room, where Mr. and Mrs. Pfunn had happily agreed to wear their Mr. and Mrs. Claus outfits.

Next in line for guest control was Kyle, who directed the newly arrived to the tinsel-adorned drinks station in the kitchen. My daughter, Clara, was in charge of beverages, and much to my amazement, she'd volunteered the minute she'd shown up this morning, sans her brooding boyfriend, Dylan.

Of course, Chris had arrived early in the afternoon to help me with last minute details.

He'd also made a point of asking me to be his date for a big New Year's Eve bash on the base.

I had happily accepted.

And much as I tried not to, I couldn't help but compare Chris to my ex. Daniel had been so threatened by my success, to the point where he sabotaged our marriage by having an affair with my friend. Yet Chris was very much the opposite.

He openly showed his enthusiasm and support for my ambitions. And he even arrived at my house with three Army Food Service Specialists to help with the cooking.

After he'd introduced the two young women and one young man, he finished with, "I expect you to give Ms. Frost the same respect that you give me."

Their response had been to stand at attention and salute me with a, "Ma'am, yes, ma'am."

The dark-haired young man said in all seriousness, "Permission to speak freely, ma'am."

I gave him a smile. "Of course you can speak freely. You're at my house, and this is going to be a Christmas party."

"Thank you, ma'am. I'm Trevor, and if I might be so bold, I believe I recognize you. Didn't you write a book about hosting Christmas parties?"

"Why yes, I did. Years ago."

His dark eyes lit up. "It's my Mom's favorite book. I learned to cook because of that book. I know those recipes by heart."

Right at that very moment, it took everything I had to keep my composure and fight back the tears that suddenly pricked at my eyes. Sure, my life the last few days had been an emotional roller coaster, chock-full of lessons and epiphanies and heartrending revelations. And though it had been an awful lot to go through, nothing had touched me as profoundly as this young soldier's words.

To think, my book had actually influenced a young person to become a cook! And a professional one at that. It was almost more than I could take.

Especially when I found out that Trevor was an incredibly good cook, too. Or rather, I should say, a good *chef*. I was absolutely amazed at the spread that he and his female companions set out, one that could rival any cooking show.

"Did you ever write another book?" he asked me as we all finished the final preparations before the party started.

I shook my head. "I'm sorry to say, but no, I didn't."

He crinkled his brow. "Well . . . why not?"

"For reasons that, when I look back, really didn't make any sense at all," I told him. "That reminds me, I have some unfinished business to take care of."

I moved over to my stovetop and reached into my pocket. Then I pulled out Daniel's letter, the one I'd found in the guestroom the night before.

The letter that had sent me into such a tailspin.

I turned on a burner of my gas stove, and touched the letter to the blue flame. I watched the flames flicker along the bottom of the envelope, setting it on fire. Then I dropped it into a pan and let it burn, until it was gone.

I looked up to see a wide-eyed Trevor watching me.

He tilted his head toward the stove. "I guess that was one of those 'reasons' you were talking about."

I gave him my most reassuring smile. "Yes, it was. And I let it get me off track for a long time. Too long. It took a good friend and some good people to set me straight again. And just so you know, I *am* planning to write a second book. Very soon."

"I can hardly wait. But hopefully you won't be putting that recipe in it," he said with a grin and a nod toward the pan.

"Not a chance." I laughed, right before I heard even more laughter coming from behind me.

I turned to see my daughter, Clara, setting up glasses with the help of another soldier, one who seemed as smitten with her as she was with him. The flashing-Christmas-light necklace that had been around her neck was now around his. Though I don't think either of them even noticed those lights. In fact, I wasn't even sure if they were aware of the world around them. Which, quite frankly, was fine and dandy with me.

The rest of the afternoon went by in a flash, and before I knew it, there I was, in my new Christmas dress greeting my guests.

My soon-to-be chaplain friend, "Tiny" Tim, waited until all the guests had arrived before getting everyone's attention and then reciting his prayer. He ended it with, "And may God bless us, every one."

Words that made me do a double take, considering my plane ride home.

After that, the party really got started, and I heard laughter and singing and just plain jovial conversation. I had forgotten how wonderful it was to be the catalyst to spread all that cheer, and to help people truly feel the Christmas Spirit.

A little while later, I stepped into Joey's game room and found him playing video games with a couple of the soldiers. As near as I could tell, Joey was being "schooled," as they say.

"Wow, you guys are really good," he finally admitted with raised eyebrows. "You must practice a lot."

"More than that," one of the soldiers replied.

"We live it," the other one said.

Which sparked an entire conversation between the three of them. I ducked out to return to the main party, all the while wondering if my son would end up joining the military one day.

Though I had to admit, I wouldn't mind it one bit. Especially after I ran into my own new Army interest looking dapper in his dress uniform. Apparently, he'd changed his clothes at some point. And while I didn't think the man could be improved upon, I now stood corrected.

In fact, I was standing in the kitchen when I noticed Chris, Kari, and Kyle suddenly huddle together. Chris flashed his high wattage smile while Kyle motioned for people to join us. Then Kari *dinged* a spoon to her wine glass, and the crowd quieted down.

"It's been such a privilege and a whole lot of fun to be invited tonight to Carol's lovely home," she announced to everyone. "I know we've all had a wonderful time at this incredible Christmas party, and I think it's time that we properly thank our hostess. So please join me now in raising a glass to Carol."

To which the entire group held their glasses high and practically shouted, "To Carol."

This was followed by Chris and the soldiers who started a chorus of "Hip, hip, hooray!"

Then the whole group joined in and cheered, "Hip, hip, hooray! Hip, hip, hooray!"

I smiled, and blinked back a few tears. I couldn't remember the last time I'd felt so happy. And so alive. Plus I'd been enjoying everything so much that I'd completely lost track of time.

"Look," I said, pointing to the clock. "It's past midnight. That means . . ."

"That's right," Chris said with a smile.

"I can't believe it," I murmured.

"Believe it." Chris moved a little closer. "Because yes, Carol, it's Christmas."

Now it was my turn to raise my glass, and so I held it high. "Let me be the first to say it. Merry Christmas! Merry Christmas to you all!"

Then the whole group joined in with wishes of, "Merry Christmas!" Seconds later, someone started to sing, "Hark the Herald Angels Sing," and everyone else joined in.

I glanced around at the crowd, and for a moment or two, I was just sure I'd caught a glimpse of my friend, Kate. The one who had started this whole ball rolling that night on the plane. And I was just sure she'd been smiling and nodding to me. Beside her, I could have sworn I'd also seen the Ghost Hosts of Christmas Past and Present.

But then I blinked, and they were gone.

Funny, but I hadn't seen the Ghost Host of Christmas Future.

Probably because my future hadn't been written yet.

Chris slid in beside me and whispered a "Merry Christmas" in my ear.

I wished him a Merry Christmas back.

Then I glanced at the twinkle lights all around, and the sparkling decorations and the artfully decorated cookies. As well as the smiling, laughing faces of all my guests, people who were here, attending a fun party, instead of sitting alone at home on Christmas Eve. Then there was Mr. and Mrs. Pfunn, who might really be Mr. and Mrs. Claus, for all I knew. Plus there was the handsome man in uniform, standing beside me.

Of all the Christmas parties I had ever hosted, I had to say, this party topped them all. It was better than anything I could have imagined.

And oh, what a Christmas this was turning out to be.

Merry Christmas!

THE END

About the Author

Cindy Vincent, M.A. Ed., was born in Calgary, Alberta, Canada, and has lived all around the US and Canada. She is the creator of the Mysteries by Vincent murder mystery party games and the Daisy Diamond Detective Series games for girls. She is also the award-winning author of the Buckley and Bogey Cat Detective Caper novels, and the Daisy Diamond Detective book series. She lives in Houston, TX with her husband and an assortment of fantastic felines. Cindy is a self-professed "Christmas-a-holic," and starts planning and preparing for her ever-expanding, "extreme" Christmas lights display every year, sometime in the early Spring . . .

www.ingramcontent.com/pod-product-compliance
Lightning Source LLC
Chambersburg PA
CBHW020630130626
46552CB00003B/1151